ARIZONA RANGER

The two Texans halted, taking in the scene. Then the taller moved forward with hands just brushing the butts of his matched guns. Halting between Bone and the drunken soldier he snapped:

"I'm a Ranger. Put down that bottle. Right now."

Bartelmo teetered on his heels, looking at the tall young Texan; then he swung the bottle up like it was a meat axe meaning to smash the jagged ends down at this rash stranger who'd come between him and his gun.

The Texan's right hand dipped faster than the eye could follow, the bar light glinted dully on the five-and-a-half-inch barrel of the Artillery Peacemaker in his palm and flame tore from the muzzle. The bottle exploded and Bartelmo yelled as chips of glass showered on him, stinging his face. The yell of pain ended abruptly as the Texan's gun whirled back to leather in a smooth move.

J.T. Edson

ARIZONA RANGER

CHARTER BOOKS, NEW YORK

ARIZONA RANGER

A Charter Book/published by arrangement with
Transworld Publishers, Ltd.

PRINTING HISTORY
Corgi edition published 1968
Charter edition/October 1988

ISBN: 1-55773-129-2

Charter Books are published by The Berkley Publishing Group,
200 Madison Avenue, New York, N.Y. 10016.
The name "CHARTER" and the "C" logo are trademarks belonging
to Charter Communications, Inc.

PRINTED IN THE UNITED STATES OF AMERICA

10 9 8 7 6 5 4 3 2 1

Roan Marrett's Son

The cowtown of Mangus, Arizona, lay half asleep under the heat of the noonday sun. Along its main and only street there was no sign of life. Just another wind and sun-dried little range town this. No great man was ever born here and no leader of the people could look back to it and call Mangus home. .

That did not mean things never happened in Mangus. They did. Like the night three weeks back, when four men broke into the Cattleman's Bank, blew open the safe and left with its contents. They disappeared without a trace and the combined efforts of the County Sheriff's office, Pinkertons and the local citizens could find no sign of the escaping quartet. This in spite of the fact that the country had been well scoured by posses, looking on all the favourite owlhoot trails.

A week after the robbery came the second big happening. Marty Candle, owner of the Candle Hotel, killed a tough Texas man called Roan Marrett. The full facts of the affair were not known, local interest being more in the recovery of the bank money. Rumour had it that Marrett and Candle quarrelled in a big stake poker game and the

Texan died of a case of slow. He was found lying on the floor of the back room, a hole in his chest and his gun in his hand; cards and money scattered around him. The sole witnesses to the affair were a gambler named Fancy and two toughs who were known to work for Marty Candle, so their testimony might have been tinged with personal bias. The matter died a death for although Marrett had been staying in Mangus for three or more months, he had never made any close friends. Even if Marrett did have friends in Mangus it was doubtful if there would be any serious investigation, for Marty Candle was not the sort of man to countenance lightly too close a scrutiny of his affairs.

Sonny Sneddon, the wizened old owner of the leather-shop, carried on much as usual, except that each day now he left his place of business around noon and walked along to where he could see the Tucson trail. There he sat for an hour or so, watching for a man he did not know. A man who might not even come.

Sonny was an old Arizona settler who had been in the country for almost fifty years, the last fifteen here in Mangus. In that time his eyes grew only a little less keen, and were still keen enough to pick up the rider who came into view over a distant rise in the trail. They were also keen enough even at that distance to make out the colour of the horse. It was a big roan. Roan horses were not common around here and this was the first Sonny had seen since the livery barn sold Marrett's big roan stallion.

The man was riding his horse with a certain, familiar, easy grace. That was obvious even though he was still too far away to be recognisable. Then Sonny Sneddon recalled the way Roan Marrett sat a horse: for all his size he'd been a light rider, easy in the saddle.

But Roan Marrett was dead.

The horse was approaching at a mile-eating lope which

brought its rider into better view at every stride. Sonny watched him all the time, studying him with the careful attention of a man with nothing useful to do with his time. He was tall, wide-shouldered, tapering to a slim waist, lithe and powerful looking. The low-crowned, wide-brimmed, Texas-style J. B. Stetson hat threw a shadow which hid his face as effectively as any mask. Around his throat, tight rolled in a riot of colour, the bandana hung its long ends over the dark green shirt almost to the waistband of the levis trousers. The cuffs of the levis were turned back, hanging loose outside his boots. Around his waist was a brown, hand-carved buscadero gunbelt, the sun glinting dully on the blued backstraps of the matched brace of staghorn handled Colt Artillery Peacemakers in the holsters.

That belt and the way the guns hung just right to a reaching hand was significant. So was the dress and riding style of the stranger. That was how Roan Marrett dressed; that was how he wore his guns.

Now the horse came alongside the porch where Sonny sat; halting, the rider looked down at the old-timer. He was, as Sonny guessed, young. His face was handsome, tanned by the elements, the eyes blue as the June sky after a storm. They were eyes which looked right straight at a man, meeting his levelly and without any hint of flinching. The face showed strength of will, intelligence and determination, the mouth with tiny grin quirks at the corners. It was a man's face. Such a face as had Roan Marrett.

Lifting his left leg the man hooked it over the low horn of his double clinched saddle and lounged there. The saddle was well-made and showed signs of much careful use. Strapped to the horn was a sixty foot Indian hair rope; to the cantle his bedroll with the warbag inside. Under the left stirrup was a saddleboot and in it a rifle. That rifle told a man things, happen he knew the West. It was a new model Winchester Centennial and not the usual weapon a cowhand carried; they preferred the lighter .44.40 Winchester model of '73. Only outlaws or lawmen went for the extra range of the .45.75 model of '76.

Then Sonny's eyes went to the boots and he felt the hair, scant as it was, on the back of his neck rising. He'd been living with Apaches for long enough to have absorbed much of their beliefs in ghosts and spirits. What he was seeing now made him believe in them. This young man was not only dressed and rode like Roan Marrett but on his expensive, high heeled boots was worked the same sort of star motif as Roan Marrett's showed.

Reaching up, the young man took out a sack of Bull Durham from his pocket with one hand, the other pushing the hat back. His hair, like Marrett's, was blond, curly. Rolling a smoke with fingers that appeared to see, he showed off the same dexterity as had Roan Marrett. Then with the smoke manufactured he spoke, his voice a soft, easy Texan drawl.

"There here the thriving township of Mangus, Colonel?"

"Yep, she be," Sonny answered, feeling an icy hand pressed on his spine. It was almost as though Roan Marrett himself sat there.

"Right peaceful looking town, man'd say," the Texan, for Texan he was, went on, his voice deceptively soft as the first whisper of a Texas blue northern storm. "Where'd a man stay, happen he was staying?"

"Hotel down there, Marty Candle's place." Sonny watched the Texan as he said the name but could read nothing on that face. "Be the best hotel in town 'cept there ain't but the one."

"Man'd likely stay on there then," the Texan was almost

talking to himself, his eyes studying the street ahead of him.

"Sure. Be you looking for somebody down there?"

"Depends on if there's anybody down there I know. Now don't it?"

The leg uncoiled from the saddlehorn and the roan started forward again before Sonny could carry on the conversation. He decided to take a chance, playing on his advancing years, to step beyond the fringe of frontier politeness and pry into a stranger's private concern.

"Didn't catch your name, friend."

"Likely," the Texan looked back, his face showing neither anger nor any other emotion at this breach of etiquette. "See, friend. I never throwed it."

Sonny watched the departing back of the rider and snorted, remembering the mocking, half polite tone Roan Marrett used when talking with him in his saddleshop. The old-timer shifted his cud of Double Strength Chewing Tobacco in his mouth and at a fair distance drowned a lizard which chanced to look out at him. With his kind action performed Sonny rose, stumped off round the side of the house and headed for the back of the hotel.

Two men sat on the rail of the hotel's coral, idly looking at the horses. They turned as they heard the footsteps and looked Sonny over with neither friendship nor welcome. One of the pair was a shortish dandy wearing a gunbelt with matched Remingtons butt forward in his holsters. The other was a big, untidy-looking, unshaven man with a Colt 1860 Army revolver shoved into his waistband.

"Howdy, Doug, Red," Sonny greeted. "Feller a feller said'd come air here."

Doug Brown scowled and replied. "You allus talk like your brain's hanging inside out."

"This feller looks real like a feller you knowed." Sonny

had this habit of making a mystery out of plain speech. "Thought you'd like to look him over."

"Why?" Red Connel grunted the word out.

Sonny ejected a stream of tobacco at one of the horses. "Might interest ye. He's real tall, wide shouldered, blond. Totes a matched brace in a buscadero gunbelt. Got him one of them new horned, double girthed Texas rigs. Talks real soft." Pausing, Sonny allowed the words to sink in. "He's afork a big roan hoss."

The change in the other two was noticeable as the words ran on. At the last five words they both jumped down from the rail, looking hard at Sonny.

"You mean—!" Brown asked.

"Yeah, he's a Texan."

Connel and Brown looked at each other: there was something in their eyes that might have been fear. They were recalling how Roan Marrett boasted of a son. A boy even more skilled with a gun than Marrett; a son who would be joining him soon.

"What're you getting at, you old goat?" Brown asked, not wanting to hear the answer he was expecting.

"Mind me a powerful lot of ole Roan Marrett."

"Marrett!" Connel spat the word out as if it left a bad taste in his mouth. "We'd best take us a look, Doug."

The Texan brought his horse to a halt in front of the Candle Hotel and swung down from the saddle. On his ride through the street he looked ahead all the time, apparently interested in nothing but where he was going. For all of that he was aware his appearance was causing a stir among the few loungers he'd passed. The general reaction was to glance at him, then look harder, eyes going from his big roan horse to him, the faces showing startled expressions. For his part his face showed no sign of even noticing that he was attracting attention. He tossed the reins over the hitching rail, leaning his shoulder against the jamb and waiting for his eyes to grow used to the cool, badly lit interior.

The desk clerk suddenly became aware that the door was blocked and looked up, his attention being to request the blocker to come in or go out. He saw the tall, lounging shape, then gulped and made a signal to the dandified gambling man who was standing just inside the gaming-room, watching a couple of cowhands playing vingt-un with a disinterested girl dealer. The gambler caught the signal and turned to look towards the door. He stiffened and the glass fell from his hand, splintering at his feet on the floor.

The clerk's eyes went back to the man at the door and felt almost relief that Fancy, the gambler, could see it too. All too often Roan Marrett had entered the hotel, stopping like that to allow his eyes to get used to the change of light. For a moment the desk clerk thought he was seeing a ghost, but the Texan was very much alive as he crossed the room and halted at the desk, hardly glancing at Fancy who'd come across to the desk and was lounging there.

Leaning on the desk the Texan glanced down at the register and asked: "Anyone in room seventeen?"

The clerk rammed his pen hard into the inkpot and swore softly as the nib broke. Then he opened his mouth and shut it again. Room Seventeen had been occupied by Roan Marrett and even now was still empty.

"No," the clerk realised his voice sounded squeaky but managed to control his tones to go on, "was you expecting someone to be there?"

"Man can never tell, Colonel. Had a friend one time who always reckoned seventeen was his lucky number. Came this way, tall jigger, toted a brace of guns and wouldn't ride nothing but a roan hoss. Allowed that was lucky for him, too. You ever see him round here at all?"

Again the clerk opened his mouth and shut it again, not wishing to give the wrong answer. Roan Marrett was always boasting seventeen was his lucky number and how his roan stallion brought him luck. However, Candle did not like people discussing Roan Marrett. He would take an even stronger dislike to anyone discussing Marrett with this soft-talking Texas man.

It was then Fancy decided he'd best help out before the fool clerk blabbed out too much.

"Sounds like you mean Roan Marrett, friend," he said. "You know him well?"

"Don't know how you mean, well," the Texan answered. "I'll take the room, Colonel. Take my hoss to the livery barn first, then bring my gear in."

The clerk looked as a ten dollar gold piece dropped on to the desk by the side of his hand. By the time he could force himself to look up, the Texan was walking towards the door.

"You never signed the register, mister," he said.

"You name it," the Texan said over his shoulder and went outside.

On the porch he stopped, hands brushing the butts of his matched guns. Two men, one tall and one short, were examining his horse, walking round the big roan and looking it over. The Texan knew the roan was a fine horse and yet it was not enough to attract such attention.

Connel and Brown circled the horse, glancing at and trying to read the brand but they were not cowhands and did not know what the burned-on scar meant. They studied the rope and the double girthed rig, then Connel glanced at the hotel porch: the way he stiffened brought Brown's attention in the same direction. They saw a pair of high-heeled, star decorated boots with Kelly spurs on them and looked up at six foot two of Texan cowhand. He stood the same way that Marrett would have stood in the same circumstances, hands near the butts of the guns, tense and yet relaxed.

Brown decided he should say something. Jerking his thumb toward the roan he said, "Fine looking hoss, friend. Right unusual rope you've got on your saddlehorn."

The Texan did not even glance at the eight plait rope strapped to his saddlehorn. "Took it off a Comanche dawg soldier on the Ole Train."

Two faces, pallid under their tan, looked at each other, neither speaking as the Texan walked by them, taking up the reins and swung into the saddle, riding on towards the livery barn.

In a hushed, strangled voice Connel gasped, "That's what Roan Marrett always said about his rope."

"Yeah and it looked just like that one," Brown agreed. "We'd best see the boss."

They both entered the hotel and found Fancy still standing at the bar and looking very thoughtful. He turned as they entered and the hope which started to kindle inside him died as he looked at their faces.

"You see him, Fancy?" Brown asked.

"I saw him." Fancy was still more shaken now. He'd been hoping against hope that Brown and Connel would scoff at the idea of this being Roan Marrett's son. "I reckon Marty will want to know about this. Come on."

They went to the door marked "Private" at the side of the desk. Fancy knocked and walked in. Marty Candle looked up, pushing the pretty blonde girl from his knee as he looked at the scared faces of the three men. He jerked his head and the girl, smoothing down her dress, walked out, passing Fancy, Brown and Connel.

"What the hell, Fancy?" Candle growled. The girl was

new here and the best looker he'd ever hired. He was a sensual man and enjoyed the privileges his hiring of girls gave him; now his pleasure was postponed.

The gambler licked his lips, then answered, "He's here."

"Who?"

"Roan Marrett's son. Just like Marrett said he would."

Candle came to his feet, six foot odd of bone and muscles, dressed in the height of frontier gambling fashion of frilly bosomed white shirt, string bow-tie, black Prince Albert coat and tight legged grey trousers with shining pointed toed shoes.

"Marrett's son?" he growled, looking from one to the other of them. "Are you sure it is him?"

"Sure enough," Fancy answered for the other two. "He acted real cagey at the desk, wouldn't give no name. But he asked if there was anybody in room seventeen. He even described Marrett and asked if we'd seen him."

"He's tall and blond, just like Marrett, got him one of them buscadero gunbelts just like Marrett's," Brown went on.

Connel reached for the bottle on the table and with a hand that shook slightly, poured out a generous drink into one of the glasses and sank it at one gulp.

"He rides one of them double rigged saddles, just like Marrett's. He's afork a roan and even got one of them Comanche ropes."

"Reckon he knows about that?" Fancy asked, pointing to the safe in the corner of the office.

"We know Marrett wrote somebody over Tucson way," Candle answered, the fear of the other three communicating itself to him. "He kept telling us his boy was coming down here to team up with him."

There was silence for a moment, every man busy with

his own thoughts. At last Candle shook himself free from his reverie and growled, "Where is he?"

"Took his hoss to the livery barn," Connel replied.

"He doesn't know I killed his old man yet or he'd be here, shooting," Candle was talking more to himself than to his men. "It must be Marrett's son and he knows a mite too much about us for our own good, if it is. Doug, trail him round town and see what he does."

The Texan rode up to the door of the livery barn and swung down to lead his horse in. He looked around the building; there were a few horses in the stalls but no sign of the owner. He was still attending to the roan when the owner came from the rear. The man stopped, staring first at the horse, then at the Texan, his face pale and his mouth dropped open. There was something like relief in his face when the Texan turned and he could see that this was a younger man.

"Howdy, I'll leave him here for a spell."

"Sure mister, sure. Leave him there, I'll get some water and a haybag for him. I'll attend to him." The owner of the barn looked at the roan's brand. "Texas brand, ain't it?"

"Hashknife outfit," the Texan replied. "Man'd say it's a Texas outfit. You all see any Texans round here?"

"Not many." The man was cautious now for he'd heard rumours about Roan Marrett's son.

"Heard about one, rode a roan horse all the time?"

Gulping, the owner took a pace back. "I've got some chores to do," he said, then hurried out to the back again.

The Texan watched him go and rubbed a hand over his chin thoughtfully. Livery barn owners, like barbers, were noted for the ability to gossip. They saw more of the comings and goings than other people and would usually find time to converse with a stranger, learning the gossip and news of other places, and passing it on to anyone who wanted to listen.

Swinging the heavy saddle over his shoulder the young man walked towards the door. He was almost out when he stopped, turned and looked at the horse. A smile came to his lips and he walked from the room, into the street, heading for the hotel.

The night was coming on when Marty Candle and his three men held another meeting in the hotel office.

"It's him all right," Brown reported to the company. "He's been going round town asking questions, never coming right out, and saying he was looking for Marrett. Nobody told him much at all. I don't even know if he's heard Marrett's dead."

"He see Sneddon?" Candle asked.

"Nope, the leathershop was closed and I never saw Sneddon all afternoon."

"All right." Candle sat back in his chair and looked at the others. "He'll have to be killed. Get him, Red."

"Me?" Connel spat the word out as if it was burning his mouth. There was suspicion in his eyes for he knew the secret of the safe and how it affected him. He also knew that Marrett had boasted the boy was even faster with a gun than Marrett himself. Red Connel knew how far he would get with stacking up against gun skill like that.

"Make it anyways you like, as long as it looks fair," Candle growled. He could see he would get nowhere with Connel on his own. "I reckon you and Doug should be able to box him in and cut him down. Fancy will be on hand, too."

Connel and Brown looked at each other. They were scared yet they both knew that they could handle the Texan if they played their cards right. Already Brown, the more intelligent of the pair, was thinking out how the killing of the Texan could be accomplished without any danger to himself or his pard.

"We'll do it tonight," he said. "And this is how we'll do it."

The Texan came down from his room, walked into the gaming room, and looked around for a moment. The room was fairly well filled with cowhands and other customers. The house girls moved amongst the crowd and persuaded the susceptible to drink more and gamble more than they meant to. No one paid any attention to the tall, handsome young man as he crossed the room and halted at the bar. He was alone at the bar, the bardog coming and taking his order for a beer, then moving away. Looking up into the mirror the Texan saw two men crossing the room: they were the same two whose interest in his horse made him thoughtful earlier in the day. He watched as they separated, one going to either side of him, standing at the bar. Then he saw the tall, thin gambling man, who'd been in the entrance hall when he registered, standing by a poker game, apparently kibitzing, but his eyes kept turning to look this way.

Connel saw Brown was in place and spoke up loudly.

"Mister, I've seed you some place afore."

The Texan turned his head towards Connel for a moment, noting before he did that the other man stood with his right hand tucked into his belt at the left side, near the butt of his gun.

"Afore and behind," the Texan answered, not raising his voice.

"Don't get flip with me," Connel growled, his hand lifting slightly.

The noise of the room died down. A man at the vingt-un

table called for a card, and it sounded loud in the room as the talk ebbed slowly away. Every eye was on the three men at the bar; every man knowing that there was going to be trouble, fast deadly trouble, very soon.

"You being somebody?" the Texan asked, his eyes on the man who stood at the other side, watching the reflection in the mirror. Then he noticed that the gambler was in the forefront of the crowd, hand held suspiciously under his coat.

"We had us the bank robbed," Connel went on, loudly, wanting to establish that here was a suspicious character. "Since then we allus asks folks their names and business here."

"Do they always tell?"

"If they want to live. Now, who are you and what the hell are you doing here?"

"Well, I'll tell you. I ain't folks and I'm minding my own damn business. Why don't you do the same?"

Connel caught the signal from Brown. His hand went up towards the butt of his old cap and ball gun. At the same moment, behind the Texan, Brown started his fast, deadly crossdraw.

The Texan's attention had not been fully on Connel, but was concentrating on Brown. Even as the Remington gun came out, swinging to line, so the Texan moved; moved in a way which took Connel and Brown completely by surprise.

Driving backwards the Texan twisted as he fell to the floor, the right hand gun materialising in his palm. He landed on his left side, facing Brown. It was a well-timed move. Brown's gun was out and lined, the hammer dropping even as the Texan went backwards. In his life Brown often boasted of his aim and he had little cause to complain at it now; his bullet would have caught the Texan in the centre of the back, right where Brown aimed it.

Only the Texan was not there.

The bullet smashed into the centre of Connel's chest even as the redhead started to draw, flinging him backwards, his old gun flying from his hand, landing and skidding across the floor.

Brown did not have time for remorse, or even to alter his aim again. Even as he shot, the Texan's gun crashed lead up under Brown's chin. The top of his head appeared to burst open. For an instant he stood erect, then crumpled down on to the floor.

Fancy saw that he must cut in and try to kill Roan Marrett's son, his only regret being that he'd waited this long before throwing in. The derringer slid from under his coat and the crowd around him scattered wildly.

The Colt derringer cracked, but a man diving for cover caught Fancy's arm and knocked his aim off. The bullet scored into the bar floor just by the head of the Texas man. He rolled over, straight on to his stomach and even as he landed he brought up his gun, fanning off three shots so fast that they could barely be told as different sounds. Fancy spun round, his derringer dropping from his lifeless hands as he crashed into the table, then slowly, almost reluctantly, he went down.

The Texan rose and looked around at the crowd, waiting for some other hostile move. Then, as the scared face of the bardog appeared over the edge of the bar where he'd disappeared at the first sign of trouble, the Texan holstered his gun.

"Thank ye, son." Old Sonny Sneddon forced his way through the crowd. In his hand he held a worn old Walker Colt that looked as if it might have been in the first ten of the Whitneyville thousand. "Didn't know how I was going to take ye until you put it away."

The Texan glanced at the tarnished deputy sheriff's badge on Sneddon's vest, then down at the worn bore of the gun. "I'll come real quiet," he replied. "A man'd likely get hisself all pizened with rust if he got shot with that relic."

"Be that right?" Sneddon growled, bristling at this slight on his prided heavyweight thumb-buster. "Well just come with me."

Marty Candle heard the shooting from his private office but made no attempt to go out and see how things were going. He was at a loss to account for the number of shots. Perhaps Red Connel paid the penalty of failure, although Candle knew Brown would try to keep his friend alive, if only to prevent his being in the minority of Candle's organisation.

There was a knock on the door and the bardog came in. With salty, range phrases that were both descriptive and to the point, the worthy explained what had happened out there. Candle was not unduly sorry to hear that his three men were dead. What bothered him was that Sonny Sneddon had taken the Texan down to the jail, a cell built at the back of Sonny's business premises.

Waving the man from the room Candle rose and set about making his arrangements for a hurried departure. His men were all dead, at least the men he could rely on were, for the other staff of the hotel were mere employees. The three men who would stand by him were gone, fallen to the guns and speed of Roan Marrett's son. The young Texan was being held by Sneddon, although held was the wrong word: there was nothing he could be held for. The shoot-out had been forced on Marrett, he'd acted in self defence. Tomorrow at the latest the Texan would be free, probably sooner, for Sonny Sneddon would not willingly go to the expense and trouble of housing a prisoner. More, knowing the suspicions Sonny Sneddon harboured, Candle was sure that Roan Marrett's son would be told who had killed his father.

Taking all things into consideration there was only one sensible thing for a man to do: leave Mangus far behind and do it as fast as possible.

Candle went to the safe in the corner of the room and unlocked it. Inside were several cornsacks. He lifted the first out and shook it gently, listening to the musical tinkle it gave forth. From the top shelf of the safe he pulled a set of saddlebags and loaded the cornsacks into them, one after the other. This was the loot from the Mangus bank; the money Fancy, Brown, Connel and Marrett stole while Candle supplied them with an alibi. This was the money Roan Marrett died for, the money which brought the deaths of the other three men.

Candle chuckled as he finished packing the bags. With Marrett out of the way the share of the loot increased. Now with the other three dead, Candle was sole surviving beneficiary. It was all very satisfying. He would have this money, could sell the hotel for he was carrying the deeds, and make a fresh start far from here.

The door opened and Candle twisted round to see who'd entered his private office without the formality of knocking. An angry curse broke from Candle's lips, for the Texan stood just inside the door, looking at him.

Studying the Texan, Candle thought how he resembled Roan Marrett with the Texas range clothing and everything. Everything? Candle tensed as that thought hit him. Of course this man dressed, talked and acted like Marrett, that was the way the Texas cowhands dressed, talked and acted. They'd been raised in the same environment, were true sons of the Lone Star State and proud of it. They wanted everyone to know that they were Texans and the rest of the world best raise their hat and talk polite around them; even the stars on both their boots were the signs of a Texas man. Candle recalled the old saying, "For a Texas man not to be wearing stars on his gear is as bad as his voting for a Republican ticket."

Almost every man of Texas used the motif in decorating his leatherwork. The fact that Marrett and the Texan here did was not surprising. Nor was the possession of the Comanche rope anything unusual. The Comanches were famous for their ropes and many a Texas man took one, if he could, from a dead Comanche warrior while trailing cattle north along the Old Trail.

Candle was seeing that there might have been a terrible mistake. This might not even be Roan Marrett's son.

"You Mr. Candle?" the Texan asked. "I came in to see you about killing Roan Marrett."

Candle cursed. He threw the saddlebags at the Texan and at the same time sent his arm up under his coat towards the butt of his gun. The Texan's hands dropped and in a flickering blur brought out the twin guns, the left throwing lead. Numbing pain smashed through Candle as the bullet caught him in the shoulder. He reeled back and saw the saddlebags miss their mark, hit the wall and fall. One burst open and a cornsack flew out, spilling money as it landed on the floor.

Sonny Sneddon and several other men rushed into the room as the Texan stepped forward and kicked Candle's gun away from his hand. The old deputy went and picked up the saddlebag, looking down into it, a happy grin on his face.

"Damn you, Marrett!" Candle hissed through his pain-tightened lips. "You'll never get that money now."

"Marrett?" The young Texan looked amused. "I'm not Marrett. The name's Waco. I'm a Territorial Ranger. One of Cap'n Mosehan's boys."

"Not Marrett?" Candle gasped the words as the town doctor came in to look at his arm. "Why did you come here acting like you was then?"

"We hit a gang who were robbing stagecoaches up Tuscan way. One of the gang was a Texas boy like me, who'd got a letter from a man down here, telling him to come along and ask for him in room seventeen at your place. We figgered that as the boy was Egan McCall the man would be his father, Roan McCall, who's wanted so bad in near every state he's been in. So Cap'n Bert sent me down here to collect him."

"You acted a mite cagey about it, boy," Sneddon remarked.

"Why sure. McCall always makes himself real popular wherever he goes. Always works with a bunch. I wasn't going to come riding in here waving a flag and shouting 'Hallelujah, I'm a Ranger,' cause if I had, somebody might say, 'Bang. I'm McCall's pard and you're dead.' I thought those two guns were in with McCall, then I saw how jumpy I was getting everybody. It wasn't until I remembered that I was riding a roan hoss, my own wanting shoeing just before I left, that I got what might have happened. Suppose something had happened to McCall and they thought I was a friend of his, folks wouldn't want to talk about it to me. Then when those three jumped me out there I knew I was right. Sonny told me you'd killed Marrett and I came on down here to tell you there was a reward out for him and that you could claim it."

Sneddon cackled delightedly. "Suspected ye all along, Marty, but I couldn't prove nothing. So I waited for Marrett's boy to come. Thought Waco here was him at first and set back to watch him stir things up a mite. You won't be needing that reward for a spell now, Marty. Reckon we was both wrong about Roan Marrett's son."

CASE TWO

The Apache Kid

"My people are not getting the food the white-eye *nantan* promised us."

The young Apache boy stood erect and proud, looking at the mocking faces of the three big white men before him.

Phil Weiland, Reservation Agent for the San Carlos Apaches, grinned at the two burly, hard-looking men at his back, then glanced at the other loungers who were looking on.

"Is that right?" he sneered. "Are you saying we starve you red heathen?"

The young Apache looked at each face in turn, reading the mockery and hatred on them. These three men who controlled the reservation and who held the key to starvation for his people hated the Apaches.

"The wagon which came from you brought only three sacks of flour and one piece of worthless meat. It was not what we were promised when we made peace with the white eyes."

Gratton, the taller and heavier of the two men, moved forward, thrusting his unshaven face towards the Apache.

"Why should we feed you damned heathen savages when the Apache Kid is up in the hills murdering white folks."

There was a rumble of approval at this from the watching crowd, for three times a white man had been found dead, killed by an Apache, and word went round blaming the Apache Kid, last, savagest and most deadly of all the Indian renegades.

"That is not the word of truth," the Apache boy shook his head. "The Apache Kid is far from here and has not been near the reservation for many suns."

Gratton lunged forward, a big fist smashing up into the boy's face, knocking him to the ground. The big man lunged forward, drawing back his foot and snarling, "Call me a liar would you?"

The boy rolled under the kick, hands shooting up and caught Gratton's foot, heaving it up into the air. The big man roared in rage and crashed over on to his back. He lit down turning the air blue with curses, his hand going to the gun at his side, drawing it.

"Leather it, *pronto!*"

The words came from Gratton's side and were backed by the clicking sound of a Colt gun coming to full cock.

Gratton obeyed the order, the tone it was given in warning him the speaker was not fooling. Then he got to his feet and turned to see who'd intervened. Three tall men stood looking at him with expressions of dislike such as he rarely encountered. One of the trio he recognised right off, the big good-looking deputy sheriff of Cochise County, Billy Breakenridge. The other two were Texans by their dress. One a tall, handsome blond boy in good range clothes, with a matched brace of Colt Artillery Peacemakers and low-tied holsters to his buscadero gunbelt. The other was not quite so tall, nor so wide shouldered: a pallid faced, studious-looking young man. His range clothes were plain, good quality and the short coat he wore had the right side stitched back to leave clear access to the ivory butt on the Colt Civilian Peacemaker in the low-tied holster at his right side.

It was the taller of the two Texans who held the gun on them, waiting for his order to be complied with, a hard twist to his lips as he went on:

"Dead game against a button."

Gratton scowled, shoving his gun back into leather again and getting to his feet. "Folks hereabouts don't take to Injun lovers."

The Texan's gun went back to its holster in a smooth flip that warned Gratton that here was master of the triggernometry arts and one who would be well able to handle the best play he, Gratton, could offer.

"And I don't take to a yeller skunk forcing a fight on a yearling button not half his size, be the young 'un red, black, white or green with blue spots."

In this raw frontier hamlet Gratton was acknowledged one of the tough citizens. He had a reputation to consider. So he considered and put aside thoughts of gunplay to end this matter as being unsafe and plain loco. There was another course left open to him.

Swinging a roundhouse punch at the Texan, Gratton expected to catch him by surprise: the only surprise was the one Gratton got. He was big and strong, but not skilled in the refinements of the fistic arts, relying on brawn. The Texan was also big and strong, and the way he acted showed he was also a skilled fist fighter.

His left deflected the wild punch over his shoulder, then his right drove with the full weight of his powerful young body right into Gratton's middle. There was an explosive grunt from Gratton, who doubled over, his face turning greyish green. On the tail of the right, and brought up with a speed which augured badly for any man who tried matching him with a gun, the Texan's left lashed into Gratton's down-dropping jaw, the knuckles landing on the jaw with a click like the meeting of two king-sized billiard balls coming together. Then as Gratton straightened out again the right came across, smashing into his jaw and spinning him round to crash into the hitching rail. For a moment Gratton hung there, then his knees buckled up and he crashed down on to his face.

Weiland stared down at Gratton, looked up at the young Texan, then at Breakenridge and shouted, "Arrest him."

"Why?" Breakenridge answered. "The way I saw it I should be taking Gratton in. What he was doing looked like attempted murder to me. This here's Waco and Doc Leroy of the Rangers."

Waco looked Weiland over in disgust as he worked his knuckles which ached from the contact with Gratton's jaw.

"We've been sent up here because your crowd at Tucson wants an investigation into the three Indian killings. Why's the hard man set on the button?"

"He reckoned we was robbing his tribe of their supplies," Weiland answered.

"And weren't you?" Doc Leroy asked.

Weiland and Dugdale, the other tough, looked at each other, then at Doc but neither took any noticeable offence at this question. That could have been because of a feeling of goodwill and Christian charity. It could also have been because in the matters of triggernometry Doc Leroy was by repute even faster with a gun than his chain lightning fast partner, Waco.

"Hell, Gratton was only fixing in to throw a scare into the Apache." Weiland was not used to backing down and the feeling hurt. "Coming here accusing us of robbing him and his bunch. These gents here," he waved a hand to the bunch of loafers who were gathered round, "saw what I sent out. So did Breakenridge."

The deputy nodded reluctantly. "I saw it. Checked it the last two times to make sure. The wagon was loaded with the right amount both times."

"I'll take your word for it, Breck," Waco answered, giving the loafers a withering look. "But I wouldn't believe this bunch happen they told me Monday came a day after Sunday."

There was an annoyed rumble in the crowd at this remark but none of them there going to make more than annoyed rumblings at a man like Waco of the Rangers.

"We supply again tomorrow," Weiland sneered. "You'd better come down and make sure we don't rob your friends."

Waco's hands took hold of the lapels of the Indian Agent's coat and dragged him forward. The young Texan thrust his face up close and in a tone as mean as the snarl of the starving grizzly said:

"Mister, I handled your hired hard man with no trouble at all. I'd expect even less with you. So don't rile me or open your mouth about me like that again. You do I'll close it with a justin, spur and all."

With a contemptuous thrust of his arms Waco sent the man staggering back and Weiland hit the hitching rail. He was angry but managed to hold down the anger and say:

"No offence, Ranger. You come and watch us load the wagon before we go."

"We'll do just that, hombre," Waco agreed, then turned back to Breakenridge. "Like to see you down at the office."

The County Sheriff maintained a small office and jail in Tannack. It was only a small place and for the most part unoccupied. Only when Sheriff Behan or one of his deputies came this way for some purpose was the building in use. It was kept fairly clean by the swamper from the saloon, although he was not strong on dusting.

Billy Breakenridge waved the two Rangers into chairs and took a seat facing them. He looked around the room, seeing that no one had been in here for some time now and promising to go and have a long talk with the swamper who was getting paid to clean up. Then he sat back and listened to Waco telling why they were here. Some of it he knew, the rest he did not.

The Apache Kid was on the rampage, or so the rumours went. Three times he struck near the San Carlos Reservation. The first time he killed a rancher and drove off his horses. The second time he stampeded a herd of cattle at a ranch house and killed the owner who came out to try to stop them. Last time it was the most infamous of all for he wiped out yet another rancher, his wife and small child. The outcry was raised by the bloodthirsty Indian-hating crowd, asking for reprisals to be taken against the Apaches and the Territory Governor to send word to Mosehan, Captain of the Rangers. The word brought Waco and Doc in from a fruitless search for an absconding bank teller and sent them to Tannack and the San Carlos Reservation.

"You all got a map of the Territory, Breck?" Waco asked at last.

"Sure." Breakenridge opened a desk drawer and took out a folded map of the San Carlos Reservation and the surrounding districts.

Spreading out the sheet Waco looked down at it, reading the map and seeing in his mind's eye the country it covered. His finger traced several water courses after Breakenridge showed him the locations of the three places where the Apache Kid made his kills.

"There's something funny about those three ranches where the Kid hit," Waco finally remarked.

Doc and Breakenridge looked at the unsmiling young Ranger. "You've got a real strange sense of humour, boy," the deputy remarked.

"Sure. I see funny things, like the Kid killing a man down here on Wednesday and being seen again on Thursday. "

"What's funny about that?"

"He was seen right over the New Mexico line, that's near two hundred miles from here. Did anybody see the Kid here. Anybody who knew him, I mean?"

"Not that I know of. I took old Scratching Jack, that half-breed tracker, out with me and he talked when he got back about a lone hand Injun. Then some damned fool started yelling about the Apache Kid. You sure it was the Apache Kid over on the border?"

"Me?" Waco looked mildly at Breakenridge. "I ain't sure of anything where Apaches are concerned. The man who saw the Kid, he was sure. He knows Apaches and knows the Kid real good. See, it was Tom Horn who saw the Kid. Would have got him too except the Kid shot his hoss from under him."

That was puzzling to Breakenridge for he knew Tom Horn well enough. Horn knew the Apaches as only a man who lived with them could. He could never make a mistake over a thing like that and would not say he'd seen the Apache Kid just for the sake of sensationalism.

"What does it mean?"

"It means the Kid either rode the fastest relay ever heard of, covered two hundred miles in a night, or some damned bronco Apache is trying to steal his reputation. You think anything about the three places he hit at?"

"No, why?"

"They control all the water in this section between them."

Breakenridge came round the desk and bent over the map, reading it and seeing that what Waco said was the truth: the three ranches would control all the water in this section and over most of the Apache reservation too.

"What do you think it means—?" he asked.

"I don't know, happen we can send a telegraph message to Cap'n Mosehan we might have a better idea."

"You can do that. Come on, I'll take you to the post office."

The following morning Waco, Doc and Breakenridge went along to the Indian Agency building and stood watching Weiland's men loading a wagon. This wagon was an eye-catching sight. Its canopy was white with the letters, "SAN CARLOS INDIAN AGENCY," painted on in two foot high red letters. The team pulling the wagon were all big blacks, fine horses from the look of them.

For a time Waco and Doc stood watching the men working. Gratton and Dugdale scowled at them but did not say anything, once was enough where they were concerned. Weiland came over with a list in his hands, offering it to Waco.

"That's what we're allowed to give them; you can see it's all there."

Waco stepped forward and looked at the sacks of flour which were being loaded. They, like the other supplies, appeared to be all right so he climbed down again.

"Looks all right this time," he remarked.

Breakenridge nodded. "It looked that way when I checked but old Chief Hawk came the next day and told me he'd not been sent his supplies."

"Those damned Indians are always lying," Weiland snorted.

"Comes of associating with you Indian Affairs men, I'd say," Doc put in, then pointed to the wagon. "Why so loud?"

"To let the Apaches know who we are," Weiland replied. "There was an agency wagon attacked by the Mimbrenos. They say they thought it was a trespasser and they went for it. The Bureau sent word that all the wagons had to be painted like this so that there was no chance of the same mistake being made."

"Stands out like a pile of coal on a snowdrift," Waco said thoughtfully, then as they walked away. "Have you ever followed them to make sure they don't change wagons, Breck, or been on the reservation when the wagon was unloaded?"

"I followed them once, kept well back so they didn't know I was following and went right to the edge of the reservation. I couldn't go any further; Cochise County ends there at the edge, so I never managed to get out and seen one unloaded. But you boys can follow it, county lines don't mean a thing to you."

"We'll do that," Waco agreed. "I hope Weiland forgets we can cross county lines and go on to the Indian reservation land."

"Who'd they sell the supplies to, if they are short rationing the Apaches?" Doc inquired. "I can't see them doing it for laughs or meanness."

"Miners in the hills, some of the rustler gangs."

"Miners, lone hand or two at most, and the Apache Kid goes for a ranch house where he's likely to hit more than he can handle," Waco remarked. "Breck, when the answer to my message gets here, hang on to it and don't let the post office man talk."

The wagon left town, headed along the well-worn trail towards the reservation, driven by Gratton, with Dugdale by his side. They did not look back but they knew they were being followed. Gratton had suggested that they get out of town and then lay for the Rangers, but Weiland squashed the idea right away. He did not doubt the willingness of his two men to commit murder, but he did doubt their ability to get away with it against Waco and his slim, deadly partner, Doc Leroy.

"Kill them," he was too wise to show doubts, "and every other damned Ranger in the Territory will be here, just looking for us and ready for war. They won't leave until they've got the men who killed their pards. And we don't want any more law round here than we can avoid."

So Gratton and Dugdale drove their wagon and told each other what they would do to Waco and Doc if they ever got them without their Ranger badges, which was futile, because a Territorial Ranger did not wear a badge. The two toughs contented themselves with the knowledge that they would fool this pair just as they had fooled the others who tried to explain away the missing supplies. The two Rangers would follow them to the end of the reservation, where their jurisdiction ended, then return to town, satisfied that the Apaches would get full measure this time.

Waco and Doc rode at an easy pace, some distance behind the wagon. They knew that Gratton and Dugdale were aware of their presence but did not let it worry them at all. The two toughs were not the kind who could worry a pair of handy Texas gents like Waco and Doc, not even if they planned to lay in wait. In fact, any lying in waiting done by the likes of Gratton or Dugdale would finish with them laying more permanently.

Riding easily afork his big paint stallion Waco looked down at the hoofmarks left by the team ahead of them. From his good friend, the Ysabel Kid, Waco had learned how to read sign and he liked to keep in practice at all times. The four horses were leaving clear sign and he noticed the off leader carried a barred horseshoe on its near foreleg. He knew that from his examination he would be able to pick out the horse amongst a dozen others.

They were drawing close to the reservation, which lay behind a section of thickly wooded country. The reservation edge was bounded by a small stream about half a mile beyond the woods.

Where the trail ran into the woods the ground took a dip and the wooded area itself thinned down to a stretch not more than half a mile wide at most. But when the wagon passed down into this dip it was out of sight.

"Let's go," Waco ordered, "I don't like that wagon being out of sight."

"Sure," Doc agreed and applied the persuasion of a Mr. Kelly petmaker to the side of his big black stallion. Before they got near to the woods the wagon was in plain view again at the other side, its team of blacks and its white, red lettered sides showing clearly against the dull reddish brown of the trail.

The reservation ford was made by the wagon even as Waco and Doc, riding at a fair speed, went through the woods. However, Waco did not want to go right up to the Apache camp so he and Doc reined into the woods and waited until the wagon came back again.

The wickiups of the Apaches were about half a mile across the border stream, a fair sized village. There were hostile looks from the men and women as the two young Texans rode in. Waco and Doc found the reason soon enough. Instead of the neat and large supply of food loaded into the wagon at Tannack only a small, miserable heap of mouldy floursacks and some flyblown meat lay thrown on to the ground.

There were angry rumblings in the crowd as the two Texans brought their horses to a halt and a short, stocky man with greying hair and the red headband of a chief came up, his face working angrily.

"I am Chief Hawk," he said in fair English. "What do you come here for?"

"We came to see what supplies the Agent sent you," Waco answered, speaking in Apache.

The Chief looked at the young man who spoke the Apache tongue, then the boy Waco had saved in town came to the side of the Chief and spoke to him quickly. Chief Hawk relaxed as he listened, then with his hand on the shoulder of the boy, said, "I thank you for saving the young one's life."

"Thanks aren't needed," Waco replied, looking at the pile of supplies. He looked at Doc, "When do you figure they made the swap?"

Before Doc could answer there was another interruption. A party of young Apache braves came into the camp with one of their number hanging across his saddle, a rough rag tied around his leg, but blood flowing freely from under it. They helped the wounded man down and laid him on the ground. Doc swung from his horse and went forward, pushing through the braves to bend down and examine the terrible gash in the man's lower leg.

"What happened?" he asked.

Through the Chief, Waco got the story. The man was part of a hunting party and had slipped into a ravine, tearing his leg on the way down. What other injuries he might have suffered were not apparent and the other braves did not seem to care. Doc bent down, finding from his examination that the man had broken a couple of ribs in the fall and that the bouncing ride on the back of the horse had not improved his condition.

"Get him inside some place," Doc ordered. The Apache braves stood still and would not obey until Chief Hawk snapped an order. "I'll fix him up, best I can, boy. You stay here for a spell."

Waco nodded in agreement at this, for he knew Doc's temper was liable to be a mite touchy when doing anything like this and was best steered well clear of until he was finished. So while Doc went to do what he could for the injured Apache, Waco strolled round the camp. The word of how he'd saved the young Apache boy in town appeared to have gone round, for there were smiles and cheerful greetings for him as he walked along.

Making for the edge of the camp Waco wondered who the boy was, for the Chief called him Son of My Brother, meaning he was adopted. Halting, the young man looked towards the woods wondering how the change had been made in there, for that was where it must have been made. Yet there had not been time to change all that food in the brief time the wagon was out of sight.

Then Waco stopped as if he'd walked into a wall. He was standing in the centre of the trail, looking down at the multitude of hoofmarks in it. Then amongst the shoeless Apache pony sign he saw the marks left by shod horses. The marks of his paint and Doc's black were there but he ignored them, for he knew them as well as he knew his own face. There were other shod horse tracks there, a team of four.

It was not the same team which pulled the wagon when

it left Tannack. The horse with the barred shoe was no longer there.

"It's as easy as that," Waco said to himself.

It was easy when a man knew what to look for. The wagon went into the woods and while out of sight came on to a second agency wagon, the change was made and the supply wagon pulled off into the woods out of sight while the replacement, with its load of near worthless food, went on. A man following at a distance would see the wagon go into the woods and at the other side see apparently the same wagon come out. The white canopy with the red letters and the team of big black horses would apparently come out again in such a short time that there would be no suspicions of it being exchanged.

Waco turned and went back into the camp, collecting his big paint stallion and leaving word that he would meet his partner in town. He rode out along the trail, this time watching more carefully. At the ford in the small stream he saw the clear imprint of the wagon team tracks and saw he was right; there was no horse with a barred shoe in the sign.

In the woods he kept his attention on the ground and soon found where the second wagon pulled off the main trail and along a smaller, almost concealed track. Since they'd gone by, someone had been busy with a piece of branch, sweeping over the tracks and obliterating any sign of where the supply wagon went. Waco took the big paint into the woods, looking for and finding a small clearing. Here he stripped the saddle and bridle from the big paint, put them under a tree and left the horse standing loose, grazing. He slipped into the woods, moving to, but not on, the trail used by the exchanged supply wagon.

He moved fast and in silence, watching the trail all the

time. Then he halted, freezing behind a tree and standing without a movement.

Ahead of him the woods opened into a large clearing and at the far side it, almost surrounded by trees, stood a small cabin. In front of the cabin were the two wagons and a couple of horses. Weiland, Gratton and Dugdale came from the cabin and stepped up to one of the wagons, looking inside. Waco dropped his hand to the butt of his gun and was about to step forward when he heard a slight noise from behind him. He started to swing round when something smashed down on to his head and everything went black.

Waco opened his eyes and groaned, shaking his head. He tried to move his hands but could not. For a few moments it did not sink into his mind that he was tied up, seated with his back to a small tree, hands lashed together behind the trunk. It was night now and in the flickering light of a big fire and the light of the moon he could see Gratton, Weiland and an Apache seated against the side of the wagon. A noise to his left brought Waco's head round. He looked at Dugdale who gave him a savage grin, then called.

"He's woke up boss."

Gratton lurched to his feet. He'd got Waco's gunbelt swung round his shoulder, and he came across and looked down at the young Ranger.

"I owe you something," he said and drew back his right foot.

Waco's left foot hooked round behind Gratton's left ankle, the right foot against Gratton's knee, then pushed hard. With a yell Gratton went over on his back, landing heavily. He came up with a snarl and lunged forward. Weiland jumped in, grabbing the man and holding him.

"Cut it out, you damned fool," he roared. "Gratton, quit it."

With all his strength, Waco kicked up, his boot smashing in between Gratton's legs, driving home with agonising and all but crippling power. Gratton gave a scream of tortured agony and doubled over, clutching his injured body. He dropped to his knees, face ashy pale and drawn in lines of agony. For a moment, Waco thought Weiland would jump him and tensed to defend himself, but the agent shook his head, stood back and told Dugdale to help Gratton back to the fire.

"Do you know why I stopped Gratton kicking you to death?"

"Sure," Waco replied, watching the startled expression on the man's face.

"You do, huh?"

"Why sure. You know that when you kill me there's going to be an investigation by every Ranger in the Territory. If there's one small slip-up they'll be on to you foot, hoss and artillery. What they'll do to you then won't be fit for a man to think about."

"I see."

"I'm going to be another Apache Kid killing, I reckon. That buck there isn't the Kid. He's the one who's been doing all the killing for you and that Eastern syndicate that's offering stocks in a cattle company that takes in most of this strip?"

Weiland's face showed more than surprise now. "You know all about that?"

"Sure. The folks running the syndicate are going to be in for bad trouble if they can't offer the land for sale. The three places the Kid made his kills at control the water hereabouts. I sent to ask Cap'n Mosehan to check on who owns the places now, or if they were sold, to find out who bought them. You're going to let the Apache kill me and make it look like an Apache Kid killing again, figger that'll rile the others of Cap'n Bert's men to say they forget anything but investigating my killing. I hope you get away with it."

"We will, don't you worry any about that. We will." Weiland rose and went to where a saddled horse stood waiting for him. He was about to mount when he asked, "How did you get on to us?"

"You've got a hoss with a barred horseshoe in one team and not in the other."

"Does your partner know about it?"

"Why sure." Waco answered cheerfully, knowing Doc was fully capable of taking care of himself.

"I don't think he does," Weiland swung afork his horse. "I'm going to town and if I think he does know I'm afraid there'll be two dead Rangers, not one."

Weiland rode off into the darkness along the trail and for a time all was silent. Dugdale sat watching his groaning partner and the Apache hunched down on his haunches, black eyes all the time on the young Ranger. Suddenly the Apache came to his feet and walked towards Waco, looking down.

"Why did you come here to the San Carlos Reservation?"

"To hunt for the man who was killing and blaming the Apache Kid."

"That is me, Toya. I killed all the men that the white-eyes say Cabrito killed."

"I knew that, the Kid is a warrior, not a killer of women and children."

The Apache grinned, his dark face flat and expressionless. "You talk well, white-eye, I will see if you can die well, too. Many times will I make you cry before I kill you. Then I will leave you at the edge of the reservation."

"One day the Apache Kid will find you, killer of women," Waco answered, his voice mocking. "Then you will cry many times."

"That day I will kill him and sell his head to the white-eye soldiers," Toya scoffed. "The Kid is a little boy fresh from horse herding. I am a warrior."

Standing up, the Apache walked away and joined the other men at the fire. Time dragged by and Waco worked desperately trying to free his hands. He knew that the Apache would be coming for him soon and wanted to have a fighting chance.

Then Waco felt something cold touch his wrist and the cords part under the edge of a razor-sharp knife. He was about to move when a hand gripped his wrist and a deep voice hissed, "Wait!"

Something hard touched Waco's hand, his exploring fingers ran over smooth wood and made out the shape of a rifle butt. Slowly he moved his hands along the wood, knowing that this was his own rifle here. He could tell by the feel for he knew that rifle well. Sitting as if he was still tied, he waited, watching the men at the fire.

Gratton got to his feet. He still looked shaken by the kick and his hatred of Waco was not lessened any by taking it. "Let's go, Toya. I want to hear him scream some afore you finish him off."

The other two rose and Waco waited, wondering if his rescuer meant to take any more part in the proceedings.

"Supaway John?" a voice called from the darkness, giving the traditional call an Indian made when entering a white man's camp looking for a handout.

A tall, wide shouldered Apache came into the light of the fire. He wore the usual buckskin shirt and trousers and the long-legged Apache moccasins. Around his head was the red band of a chief and across the crook of his arm he held an old Winchester 66 carbine.

Gratton and Dugdale looked at the Apache with no great interest, for they were used to having Indians come in like this begging for food. Toya stared at the other Apache for a moment, then with his hand grabbing for the old Dragoon revolver in his waistband, he shouted:

"The Kid!"

Like a rattler striking, the tall Apache moved. His old yellow boy flowed from the crook of his arm and levered three shots into Toya's belly so fast the reports merged into one blurr of sound and movement. It was done so fast that neither Gratton nor Dugdale had a chance to make any move at all.

Waco came to his feet with a bound, hand gripping the Winchester at the small of the butt and throwing it forward. His hands were stiff but he still moved fast enough. Held hip high the heavy rifle roared, throwing a four hundred and five grain flat-nosed bullet into Gratton's body, knocking him off his feet and into Dugdale even as he was trying to throw down on the Apache Kid.

Round swung the muzzle of the carbine and spat, once. Dugdale rocked backwards, a hole between his eyes.

Flipping open the lever of his rifle Waco walked forward and rolled Gratton on to his back. The man was as dead as one could be with what appeared to be half of his right side blown away. Looking up at the Apache Waco nodded and said:

"My thanks, red brother."

"You saved my brother's life, Ranger," the other replied in a deep throated growl. "Your friend saved an Apache in the village. I have repaid my debt to you."

Waco bent and took up his gunbelt, checking that the guns and holsters were not dirty. When he looked up again he was alone with the three bodies. The Apache Kid was gone in complete silence. Waco lifted a hand in a silent tribute and then turned and went back along the tracks, looking for his horse.

"I tell you, boys," Weiland looked at the crowded saloon in the cold grey light of dawn. "We've got to do something about these Apaches. The Ranger who went out to the reservation is dead. I found his body out there, just over the reservation border."

Doc Leroy looked up, his face showing none of the anxiety he was feeling: Waco should have been back long before now. Of course the young man could look after himself and would stick on to whatever he found until he followed it to an end, and somehow Doc could not bring himself to believe anything could happen to Waco. He also did not believe that Weiland had found his pard's body and left it where it was to prove the killing took place on the reservation.

"You said wait until dawn, Ranger," a man spoke up. "It's near enough dawn right now. If the Apache Kid is around here he must be hiding with them Apaches on the reservation. Now I don't say as how we should go in there shooting, but I allow we ought to take a posse out there, see if your pard is dead or not and then search every wickiup in the village."

There was a rumble of approval at this from the other men. They'd been here most of the night and Weiland's arrival nearly sparked off trouble. Doc and Breakenridge were now trying to hold the men from going out to the reservation and either searching or attacking the Apaches.

"You know what'll happen if you try it, Neal," Breakenridge put in. "They won't let us make the search and there'll be shooting."

"And then the Apaches'll be cleared off that reservation by the Army," Doc went on. "Throwing all that land open for sale."

"Is that bad?" the man called Neal asked. "I could use some more land."

"You won't get it. An Eastern syndicate is selling shares in a land and cattle company out there that covers every inch of reservation, including those three spreads where the Kid hit and damned near all of the neighbouring ones."

Neal looked at Doc for a moment. He was a rancher, running a small place on the edge of the reservation. "I ain't selling my place."

"Mister," Doc sounded mocking. "You won't need to sell out. They've already bought the three places and those three—"

"Control all the water." Neal did not need that explained to him.

"That's right," Breakenridge agreed. "They control all the water. The only thing that's stopping them moving right in and taking over is that Apache reservation. If the Apaches are driven out that land is offered for sale. The land company gets it. Just you boys think about that."

"What's all that mean?" another man asked.

"It means, friend, that those Eastern company men need the Apache land. When they get it they can force every one of you out of your places. They've already started to sell shares in that company—"

"I don't know how you can stand there talking when your pard is laying dead out there on the reservation."

"Gents," the voice came from the door. "You're looking at the best looking ghost in Arizona."

Weiland and every man stared at the door. The Indian Agent recovered first. He leapt down from the table where he'd been arguing with the crowd and ran across the room to the other door, throwing it open. Then he screamed. Outside stood a tall, wide shouldered Apache Weiland knew all too well.

Slamming the door Weiland hoped to save his life, but from outside the Winchester carbine cracked twice, two holes leaping in the wood. Weiland stood erect for a moment, then turned and crashed down on to the ground.

The other men came to their feet, shouting and drawing guns. Waco's voice cut over the noise, bringing silence to the crowd.

"All of you, listen to me. The Apache Kid didn't kill those three men. A buck called Toya did it. He's dead, so are Gratton and Dugdale."

"So?" a man asked, jerking a thumb towards the door. "Let's go after that Apache who just downed Weiland."

"Why sure," Waco replied, "go right ahead. That was the Apache Kid. He saved my life and killed Toya."

There was a lamentable lack of willingness amongst the men to go after the Apache Kid. Not one of them wanted to go out there first in case the Kid was waiting in ambush.

"The Kid didn't do the killings; he couldn't have killed the Randals," it was Breakenridge who spoke. "From what Waco told me I sent a wire to Tom Horn. He saw the Kid over near the New Mexico line morning after the Randals died."

Every man here was a horseman and knew that horse or relay team was never foaled which could run that distance in the hours of one night.

"What're we going to do now, Waco?" Doc asked. "The Kid's sign is fresh out there."

"We were sent to get the man who killed those three. We got him. Let some other team hunt for the Kid. He saved my life and I owe him for that."

A Man Called Drango Dune

Waco rode into the small mining town of Allenvale, sitting easily in the saddle of his big paint stallion and looking around with some disgust. He rode slowly and whistled a cowboy tune as he held the horse to an easy walk.

The young Ranger was riding along and doing a job which did not greatly interest or please him. It was something he would rather not be doing at all, and if left to his own devices, would have left undone.

A few weeks before, along with his slim, pallid and very able partner, Doc Leroy, Waco broke up the hold-up of a private stage coach carrying bullion from a mine near Allenvale. It was just a routine piece of work for them, two of the gang were dead, one badly wounded and the other two making hair bridles in Yuma. Then a message was received from the owner of the mine, Frank Allenvale, requesting that the men who had saved his money be sent to Allenvale so he might reward them.

Such a request at another time might have been ignored, but the Governor of the Territory sent along a request that one of the two men responsible be sent along. Waco was still not sure whether Doc arranged the cards when they cut or not, for his nine was beaten by Doc's jack and he rode out.

Now he was riding slowly along Allenvale's main street and not wanting to get to his destination. He asked for no reward for doing this work, nor did Doc Leroy; they saw what they had to do and did it.

The sign over the door of a shop caught his eye as he rode past and he swung the big paint round in a circle to get down. Over his head the store sign announced to the world, "Henry D. Hawken, You Want It, I've Got It."

Swinging down from the saddle of the big paint stallion, Waco tossed the reins over the hitching rail and walked into the store, halting just inside the door and looking around. The owner was almost justified in his claim, for there was almost everything a man could need on view and for sale here. Rifles were racked against one wall, a case of revolvers showed at the side of the room; there were clothes, cooking utensils, canned foods, mining implements and a vast assortment of other goods all neatly arranged.

The owner of the store was busy when Waco came in. He sat on a clear space of the counter, a small, fat, happy-looking man of indeterminate age, dressed in a collarless white shirt and black trousers. Around him were ten or more young children, all eagerly listening to him talking. Waco crossed to look in the gun case and listen to the story. At the age of those kids he'd been running wild in Texas, not being told fairy stories.

"Well now," the little fat man at the counter said to his enthralled audience. "The beautiful princess woke up when the handsome prince kissed her. She looked up at him and said—"

The door opened and two men came in. Both wore range clothes but they were not cowhands. Waco's experienced glance told him that. They were hard-faced, tough-looking men wearing low tied guns. One was a man Waco's size, the other shorter and vicious-looking. Both were alike in their cold, hard eyes and arrogant, sneering ways.

The taller of the pair glanced at Waco then snapped. "All right, Hawken. Stop your fooling and get over there."

"Yeah, move it," the other went on. "We ain't got all day. Mr. Allenvale's down at the saloon waiting for us."

They started forward and Waco moved to block their way, his voice gentle yet menacing as the distant rumbling of a storm.

"You just set back and wait, I like the story."

The big gunman's hand reached out for Waco's shirt, his other fist pulling back. Then he let loose and howled, hopping on one leg, the other gripped in his hands, for Waco raked his Justin down the shin bone hard. In the same instant Waco's right fist shot out, smashing full into the face of the man and knocking him back across the room to crash into the door.

The other man lunged forward, hand fanning down towards his hip.

"Try it!" Waco's flat snapped offer was backed by the appearance of his twin Colt guns, produced with a speed many boasted of but very few attained.

The man stood fast. His friend hit the door hard and hung there; through his dazed mind came the thought that here was a man he should have steered well clear of. He put a hand up to rub his chin, then snarled:

"You're some handy with a gun for a cowhand."

"I'm not bad for a Ranger either; the name's Waco."

"Waco of the Arizona Rangers," a freckle-faced, red-haired youngster who'd been seated away from the other children and looking bored at the story, yelled. "Boy, it's really him."

Waco holstered the guns and the two men stood fast, neither wanting to take things up with a man like Waco of the Arizona Rangers. There were others who had tried it, some of them were dead, the others never tried twice.

"You say your boss was down at the saloon?" Waco asked.

"You going to arrest him, Waco?" the red-haired yelled eagerly.

The taller gunman snarled out a curse. Waco turned his cold blue eyes on the man and warned, "You talk clean round kids, *hombre*."

"That kid annoys me," the man replied.

"He'd be about your size I reckon." Waco turned his attention to the boy and smiled, "Should I arrest him, boy?"

Hawken's face worked nervously; he came forward and put his hands on the shoulders of the boy and said, "Go on home, Johnny. Take the rest of the children with you. I've got some work to do."

Reluctantly the boy called Johnny started to usher the others out. The taller gunman stepped forward and looked at Waco.

"I'm Mr. Allenvale's foreman."

"Boss gun's more like," Johnny yelled and darted out of the door.

"One day I'm going to get that kid and quirt manners into him."

Waco looked the man up and down with disgust and replied, "You try it while I'm around and you'll end up picking my Justin out of your mouth. You get what you want, then we'll go down and see your boss."

"Sure, Ranger. I'm Magee, this is Talbot."

Waco ignored the offered hands, turning to the counter. "Take me a box of forty-fives," he said. "Don't reckon you stock the new Winchester shells yet?"

"No call for them up here," Hawken answered. "Could I

serve these two gents first, I keep my ammunition locked away."

"Why sure," Waco glanced down at the small man's hands; he always looked at a man's hands when first meeting him. What he saw made him look harder at this small, cherubic-looking man who told fairy stories to the children. "Serve ahead."

"Take a sack of Bull Durham," Magee growled. "Pay you for it next pay day."

With a sigh Hawken handed over a sack of tobacco and then served Talbot who also promised to give the money over on the next pay date. Then as the storekeeper went into the back room, Magee turned and opened his mouth.

"Don't wait for me," Waco said before the man could speak. "I'd as soon not be seen on the streets with the likes of you."

Magee opened his mouth again, angry words rising then falling unsaid. His boss wanted to see this Ranger and would not like the idea of his being roughed up. There was also the possibility that Waco himself would not care for the roughing up and would make his objections with the same speed and handiness he'd already shown. With this in mind Magee turned and walked from the room, followed by Talbot.

Hawken returned with a box of cartridges in his hand; he handed it over and while making change for the note Waco gave him, looked at the young man.

"I wouldn't pay any attention to what Johnny says."

"Man'd say he doesn't like Allenvale."

"He doesn't."

"What's eating him then?"

"A man doesn't talk much against Mr. Allenvale, or what happened to Pete Bren, Johnny's father. The boy has ideas but there is not proof at all."

"What about?" Waco watched the man all the time.

"Like I say, a man doesn't talk much in this town," Hawken did not meet Waco's eyes. "Magee and his kind are hired to see to that."

"Didn't think they'd bother *you*," Waco looked at the storekeeper's right hand as he spoke. "Waal, it's not my affair anyhow. Thanks for the shells, *adios*."

The sun was dropping as Waco stepped out into the street and looked around. Like most of these small towns all the businesses were on the main street; the jail and marshal's office lay just a little bit farther along from the saloon. Waco swung into the saddle of the paint and headed first to the livery barn where he made arrangements to leave the horse and his gear. He also fixed up to sleep in the spare room of the barn for he did not want to stay in a hotel.

The saloon was not crowded when Waco entered, and he could tell at a glance which of the men was Allenvale. Not that Allenvale was a big man; he stood at most five foot nine, but he was wide shouldered, hard-looking under his expensive eastern-style suit. His face was reddened by the sun, hard and arrogant, the face of a man who knew power but not friendship. He would never make men follow him through admiration but always by driving them.

At the bar he dominated the conversation and the group of lesser men who were around him, listening to their words as long as they were not opinions contrary to his own.

The other men, apart from Magee and Talbot, made a varied selection; a few townsmen, three who might be mining men from the east, a whisky drummer and an old desert-rat prospector, the sort who made his living prospecting, trying for the big strike, the mother lode.

The others of the crowd were the usual kind of saloon loafers, but all were listening with polite attention when Allenvale spoke, laughing at his jokes and treating him with the deference Allenvale felt he deserved.

Magee saw Waco and interrupted his boss, "The Ranger's here, Mr. Allenvale."

Allenvale looked at the tall young Texan who came across the room and held out a hard, work-roughened hand. "Howdy son," he said. "Are you the Ranger? Where's your partner? I told Mosehan to send you both along."

"*Cap'n* Mosehan figured one of us would do," Waco placed some emphasis on the first word, "when you wrote the Governor and asked for us to come."

The smile died for an instant and there was an uncomfortable silence among the other men. All eyes were on this tall, wide-shouldered young Texan man who spoke back in such a manner to Mr. Allenvale.

For a moment the miner stood silent, not knowing quite what to make of this. Then he laughed and waved his hand to the bar.

"Step up and have something. I always like to reward good work, so here." He took out a wallet and extracted five one hundred dollar bills without even making an impression on the pile left. "I reckon you and your partner will have you a time with this."

"Likely." Waco accepted the money and thrust it into his pocket. The reward was going to the widow of a Ranger killed in the line of duty, but he did not tell Allenvale that. "Well, thanks, *adios*."

"You're not going, are you?" Allenvale growled. "Here, Joe, a drink for the Ranger. Hell, you've only just arrived."

Waco remembered that Mosehan asked him to be polite to Allenvale who was getting to be a political power in the Territory. He turned back to the bar and replied, "I'll take a beer then."

"Beer?" Allenvale snorted. "Is that the best you can do? Make it whisky for the Ranger."

"Beer, Mister," there was no friendliness in Waco's tones. "I learned real young that whisky gets a man no place in a hurry."

Allenvale eyed the youngster, about to make some remark about his youth. There was something in Waco's eyes which stopped the words unsaid. For once in his life Allenvale felt uneasy, knowing that here was a man with no respect for either his money or his power.

"How come only the one of you came?" Allenvale asked. "Couldn't Mosehan spare the two of you?"

"He couldn't spare one of us, but the Governor asked real friendly. So Doc and me cut the cards for who came."

"And you won?"

"Lost."

Again there was that sudden silence, the other men moving slightly away from Waco as if wishing to show clearly they were not with him at all. Allenvale was angry and suddenly he wanted to show this unsmiling young man that he was the real power of this town, that he ruled here and no man could say a word to him.

"How'd you like the town?" he asked.

"Didn't see much of it yet."

"I built it right here, so's it'd be good and handy for me and mine. Do you know something, Ranger, this town is built on an Indian reservation." Allenvale looked at the other men for corroboration of the statement; they all gave their complete agreement. "Sure, I built it on the reservation because this was the best site for a town in miles. Anyways, the Indian Affairs Bureau said I couldn't so I went right on ahead and did it. Yes sir, this is my town, Ranger."

Before Waco could reply a tall, fattish, well-dressed man entered. He came to the bar and was introduced as

Judge Holland, the local court official. He was just as clearly Allenvale's man as the others. The judge was cool and distant, obviously regarding Waco as no one in particular: just a whim of Allenvale's and therefore someone to be barely civil to. Waco regarded the judge as a pompous troublecauser who would only follow the law as long as the law followed Mr. Allenvale.

Other men came in, and the talk became general. Waco noticed that although all appeared to be for Allenvale, there was a lack of warmth in their laughter. The town marshal, made a brief appearance, a tall, slim man just past middle age.

"Ranger," Allenvale said, "come and meet our marshal, Dan Thorne."

"Howdy Dan." Waco held out a hand. "I heard Hondo Fog talk about you."

Thorne's face flushed slightly at this. He was once known as a real fast gun lawman, honest, brave and the tamer of bad towns. Now he was here in a small Arizona settlement, holding down a job that years before he would have assigned to his newest deputy.

"Sarah Shortbow came to see me yesterday," he said.

The miner's face darkened in a scowl. He turned his back on Thorne and called for a round of drinks. For a moment Thorne stood looking at Allenvale's back, then he turned and walked out of the room. Waco watched him go, realising that Allenvale owned more than just the town of Allenvale.

"Say, Ranger," Allenvale boomed from the bar. "I can always use a good man or two. How'd you and your partner like to come and work for me. I'll pay top rate."

"We're hired and we like the boss," Waco replied.

"Huh! Like I say I can always use good men. You the fastest with a gun?"

Waco shook his head. He was getting to like Allenvale less all the time. "I know three who can shade me."

"Who are they?"

"My partner, Doc Leroy, is the fastest man I ever saw with a single gun. Ole Mark Counter, he can shade me with either hand."

"And the other?"

"Dusty Fog. The man doesn't live who can touch him with two guns."

There was a rumble of assent at this, for the three men named were all well-known as being skilled exponents of the art of grab and shoot. The whisky drummer spoke up, "I was in Dodge when Dusty Fog brought that Rocking H herd in. He surely made Earp and Masterson hunt their holes that time."

"Not in Dodge he didn't," the bardog objected. "Weren't neither Earp nor Masterson in Dodge when the Rocking H came in. They'd both left on business."

There was a guffaw at this. Earp and Masterson had been called away on urgent business at other times when dangerous men came looking for them. The bardog was a Kansan and proud of the lawmen who ran his cattletowns for him.

"Wyatt's no slouch," the bardog affirmed.

"Masterson's better," another man put in.

Waco leaned back and listened to the conversation which walled up around him at this statement. It was one he'd heard many times before, in many a town from Texas north to Kansas and west to Arizona. Wherever men gathered in a bar the subject was likely to turn to gunfighters, arguments as to who was the best, the fastest and the most accurate. Every man held his own particular hero and was willing to boast that the said hero was faster than any other, better than any other. Even if there was no chance of it ever being proved one way or the other.

At last the old prospector spoke up, his cracked old voice coming in a lull. "You're all forgetting the best of them all. A man who could have shaded all these so-called fast men today. He was the law in Newton and Sedalia just after the war, his name was Drango Dune."

The others all looked at the old-timer and Allenvale laughed, then said, "You're going back there some, Sam. That was in the cap and ball days. Don't reckon any of us ever met him."

"I did, knowed him real well. I'll never forget him, most unlikely cuss I ever did see. Him being so tough, didn't look like he was but I saw him whup a railroad man twice his size. Fast, mister, he was the fastest I ever saw with that ivory handled Dragoon gun."

"Dragoon pistol," Magee snorted. "I never saw a man use one, that amounted to anything. They're too heavy."

Waco thought of his very able friend, the Ysabel Kid who not only carried and swore by a Colt Dragoon but also proved time and again that Colonel Sam's old four pound thumb-buster was a weapon to be feared in capable hands. However, the young Ranger did not say anything; he was looking at the door and saw Henry Hawken outside. The storekeeper had been about to enter when the old prospector started talking. He stopped outside, looking in at the group for a moment, then turned on his heel and walked away again.

"What happened to Drango Dune in the end?" a man asked.

"He was fighting a bunch of owlhoots one night. Heard a noise on the roof above him, turned and shot down one of his deputies who'd gone up there against his orders. He broke that gang but threw in his star; wouldn't wear it again after he dropped his own man. I don't know where he went after that but I sure won't never forget him and I reckon I'd still know him."

The talk went on and after a time Waco left the bar; none of the men noticed he'd gone. He went along to the marshal's office and opened the door. Thorne sat at the desk, head in hands. He looked up as the door opened.

"Howdy Ranger."

"Howdy, I'd like to stay on here for the night if I can."

"Sure, make yourself at home. You eat?"

"Not for a spell." Waco looked round the small office.

"Come on across to the Bren place, they won't be closed yet."

"Bren, I've heard that name before."

"Not around town you won't have. The widow runs it now. Her husband met with an accident out at his mine." Thorne looked straight at Waco. "An accident."

"Why sure, except that now Allenvale owns the mine."

Thorne looked at Waco, his face working, then at last he said, "I investigated the accident. It was an accident from all I could find. Who talked?"

"The boy mentioned he didn't like Allenvale. It's none of my worry, I'll be riding back to Tucson come morning."

Waco led the big paint stallion from the livery barn out on to the street and looked around for a moment. He did not like this town of Allenvale; there was an unhealthy look about it, like a town living in fear. The people here hated and feared Allenvale yet accepted him as their lord and master.

Two men rode into town; Waco watched them without interest, not knowing or caring who they were. He might have made a guess at one of them, the tall, handsome and expensively dressed young man afork the magnificent palomino gelding. From his dress, the costly, silver decorated saddle and the arrogant look about him Waco guessed this was Dinty Allenvale, son of the miner. The boy was not at the saloon the previous night, but Waco had heard some mention of him.

Dinty Allenvale it was, and in a vile mood. Even at this early hour he was more than half drunk. The gunman who rode at his side was not sober either, for they had been hitting the bottle on the way into town.

Stopping his horse Allenvale pointed ahead to where a pretty, black haired, dark-skinned girl was walking towards the saloon. She passed Hawken and Johnny Bren, greeted them, and carried on along the sidewalk. Allenvale reached down, unstrapped the rope from his saddlehorn and headed for the girl, riding fast. His rope built up into a noose and shot out to drop over the girl's head and tighten round her neck. The horse lunged by and the girl was jerked viciously from her feet. She hit the ground hard, her limbs jerking once, then lay still.

Waco came forward fast; Allenvale was off his horse and bending over the girl, looking down at her. From the way her head was bent over Waco knew she was dead, her neck broken. Allenvale looked up truculently. Waco was moving in fast, seeing faces at windows watching him, and that Hawken had shoved Johnny Bren into the store before coming forward.

"She's dead," Waco said softly.

"So what?" Allenvale sniffed. "Who the hell—"

"I'm a Ranger. Hand over your gun. I'm arresting you for murder."

"Hear him, Kenny boy, just hear the man," Allenvale sniggered. "He said that real nice—!"

Waco's fist shot out, smashing into Allenvale's sneering face and knocking the young man down. At the same moment the gunman started to draw, his gun coming out of leather as Waco turned. There was the crash of a shot from the gun which came into Waco's right hand; the gunman jerked up in his saddle, his gun falling from his hand. The horse bucked and the man slid down to hit the ground hard and lay still.

Holstering his smoking gun Waco dragged Allenvale to his feet and half pushing, half carrying the dandified young man brought him to the jail. Thorne came to his feet as the door of his office burst open and a figure was thrown in, crashing to his knees by the desk.

"What the hell, Ranger?"

"I'm arresting him for murdering a girl out in the street there," Waco answered. "Open the cell door."

"But that's Dinty Allenvale."

"So?"

"He's Allenvale's boy."

"Mister, I don't care if he's Robert E. Lee. He killed a girl out there and I'm holding him for murder."

"Which girl?" Thorne asked, his face working.

"Dark haired girl," Waco replied. "Are you opening the cell or do I?"

"You stop him, Thorne, do you hear me, stop him!" Dinty Allenvale yelled. "Tell him to let me loose."

"I can't let you lock him up, Ranger," Thorne said.

"The keys are in the door," Waco replied. "The only way you can stop me is to kill me."

Thorne stood back, watching the young Texan drag Dinty Allenvale to his feet and shove him into a cell, then lock the door and pocket the key. Then when Waco came back into the office said:

"If I was you I'd be long gone from this town by the time Allenvale hears about this. He won't set back and leave his son in jail."

"He will. Who was the girl?"

"You say she was dark haired?"

"Sure, looked like she might have some Indian blood in her."

"Sarah Shortbow, she's half Apache. Is she dead?"

"Got her a broken neck," Waco answered. "It was murder. I never thought to hear Dan Thorne talking like this."

"Didn't huh?" Thorne looked at Waco. "Hondo Fog told you about me: how I cleaned up the bad towns. Sure I did, then one night I heard Clay Allison was coming to town looking for me. I got to thinking about it and I got scared. I sweated it out all night. Next day I let out of town and didn't come back for a week. Then I learned it was all a joke, Allison was nowhere near. It finished me as a lawman. Other towns heard of me and I drifted on, then Allenvale took me on here. I knew that I was working for him and I took on just the same. Son, I was scared then, I've been scared ever since. That's why I want no part of this now."

"You've got no part of it. I've taken the prisoner and I'm holding him here. You can't do a thing about it."

"Do you think you can keep him for trial, or even get witnesses to come out and talk against Allenvale, in this town?"

"Mebbe."

"Go out there in the street and try."

Waco went into the street. The crowd who had gathered round the body of the girl, parted and let him through. He looked at them; people who had been looking through windows or from their doors and had seen what happened.

"Who saw what happened?" he asked.

There was silence now, faces turning from his eyes, then slowly the crowd broke up. Waco's cold voice halted them. They turned, not meeting his contemptuous gaze.

"Some of you saw what happened and know what happened. I'm holding Allenvale for trial. If he gets off through lack of witnesses, don't any one of you ever leave this town again. If you do I'll see to it that every lawman in the territory knows what happened and if you as much as spit on the sidewalk you'll wind up in jail."

"You can't talk to us like that," a man growled.

"I'm doing it. I'm talking to you like a pack of cur dogs. You're all hawgscared that Allenvale won't let you live here any more if his son comes up for trial. I'm going to see he gets tried, even if I have to stand alone."

The crowd scattered, only Hawken and a grizzled old-timer staying with the body. Neither of them looked at the Ranger or spoke as he turned and walked back to the jail.

"I told you," Thorne said as Waco came in. "Nobody in this whole town's going against Allenvale. The Judge won't even let it come to trial. He'll say the girl was just a half-breed chippy——"

"Sure, she's an Indian," Waco agreed, then he remembered something Allenvale had said the previous night. "Is this town built on an Indian reservation?"

"Two miles inside the boundary line. I remember there was some trouble over it at first——"

"I've got to send a message." Waco turned on his heel. "I'm holding you responsible for keeping my prisoner. If he's gone when I get back I'll hold you for trial."

There were sullen glares for Waco as he walked through the streets, making for the post office. He ignored them, for a small matter like personal popularity never gave him the slightest worry. He entered the post office and taking a telegraph message form wrote on it.

"I can't send this, Ranger," the owner of the office gasped as he read what was on the form. "Mr. Allenvale would have my job."

"And I'll have it if you don't," Waco answered. "There was a postmaster in another town refused to send a message for a territorial Ranger, and he was within a fortnight of retiring on pension. Mister, they fired him out without a dime. You've got your choice, do you send it, or do I?"

"Do you understand Morse code?" the man asked and Waco nodded. "I may as well send it then. But I want protection."

"Mister, you'll get it." Waco agreed, but he stayed to make sure the message was sent correctly.

On his way back to the jail Waco called in at Hawken's store. The fat man was behind the counter, his face showing worry as Waco came up.

"Doc and I took the girl to the undertaker's," Hawken said.

"You see what happened?"

"I see it, me and half the town. I thought this might happen, or something like it. You see, Sarah was going to have a baby. It didn't show yet. Young Allenvale was the father."

Waco stood silent for a moment, then asked, "I need witnesses, how about it?"

"You won't get any in this town."

"I figgered on one and I don't want to have to call young Johnny."

Hawken was silent for a time, then he looked at Waco. "This place is my home. I can't go against Allenvale and stop on here, you know that."

"I didn't think that would stop *you*."

Waco turned and walked out of the store. Hawken watched the young Ranger go and thought of the emphasis placed on the last word. Either that shrewd young man knew something or he was a remarkable guesser.

• • •

Allenvale and eight of his men came into town shortly after noon, thundered along the main street and halted in front of the jail. "Thorne!" Allenvale roared. "Thorne, come on out here."

Dan Thorne stepped out of the office. Waco picked up a shotgun from the rack, broke it, and thrust in two shells, then snapped the breech closed and followed. He halted on the porch and waited for Allenvale to say something.

"You've got my boy in jail, Thorne, I want him out and fast."

"He's my prisoner, the marshal hasn't a thing to do with it," Waco replied. "I'm holding your son on a charge of murder."

"Murder?" Allenvale snarled. "Why she was nothing but a half-breed chippy and it was an accident what happened out there. My boy wasn't doing anything wrong. She's only a damned Indian. I'll send Judge Holland along to see you."

"That won't get your boy loose. Like you said, the girl is an Indian and this is an Injun reservation we're standing on."

Allenvale scowled, not understanding the significance of the statement just made. "Do you think you can pull this?"

"I already have."

"One man against the town. Who'll help you?"

"My partner and every other Ranger." Waco watched the men.

"How're you going to send for them?"

"I already have. I sent off a telegraph message and if any of your men lay a hand on the man who sent it I'll kill them."

"We're eight to one," Allenvale answered.

"Sure, if that's the way you want it, cut loose your dawgs, and let's hear them howl."

The gunmen tensed. They saw the shotgun on the young man's arm and knew that he would empty both barrels before they got him. Some of their number were going to be killed, and killed in a messy manner, if they started. Allenvale knew the same thing but where some of his men might not know they would be hit he knew that he was the Ranger's first mark. He would get the first barrel of that shotgun into him.

"No shooting, boys," he warned. "Let's go down to the saloon and talk with the Judge. He'll soon straighten this out."

Waco pulled the money Allenvale had given him from his pocket, screwing it up and throwing it up at the man. "I was fixing to give this to the widow of one of our boys. I don't think she'd want it."

There was red rage in Allenvale's eyes as he watched the money fall to the street. Without a word he turned his horse and rode down the street followed by his men. Waco turned to walk back into the office when he heard a yell from Thorne and was pushed aside. At the same instant a shot sounded and he came whirling round.

One of the men at the rear of Allenvale's party had drawn a gun, brought his horse round and shot. Only the push given him by Thorne saved Waco's life. The marshal was down holding his leg and the gunman tried to line his gun afresh.

Waco dived forward, off the sidewalk, landing on the ground and firing the shotgun. At the first roar the man rocked backwards, clean out of his saddle. The other men turned in their saddles to look but none of them made a move; they just rode on towards the saloon.

Coming to his feet Waco vaulted back on to the sidewalk and helped Thorne into the office again. The man was hit in the leg and Waco started to do what he could.

"I couldn't let them gun you like that, boy," Thorne said. "Reckon I've worn a law badge too long."

"I'm real pleased you have," Waco answered. He spun round with his gun coming out of leather as the door opened.

"Easy there, boy." It was the grizzled old man who'd helped Hawken with the girl's body. "You're too fast with your gun to suit me. I ain't had so much work since the mine caved in. Let's have a look at that leg."

Thorne lay back in the chair and looked at the door which led to the cells. "That lousy spoiled rat. He'll never forget that punch you gave him, even if that's all he gets for killing the girl."

"He'll get more than that," Waco promised. "There's been a big shake-up at the capital. The Governor cleaned house, got rid of all the crooked bunch and brought in good, straight men. He won't stand for any play like this. Did you see what happened to the girl, Doc?"

"No, I ain't even sure I'd talk if I had seen it. The other folks aren't going to talk either. Allenvale has them all buffaloed."

Waco looked down at Thorne's wounded leg and smiled. "Not everybody. Who's this coming along now?"

The door of the jail opened and Judge Holland came in, followed by three other influential men of the town.

"I have come to order the release of the prisoner," Holland said pompously. "Let him out, young man."

"Nope."

"As judge of—!" Holland began.

"This town doesn't come into it at all, Judge. I'm holding Allenvale for the murder of an Injun on the reservation."

Holland knew what Waco meant right straight off. His

face went even more red and he snapped. "You mean you are holding him on a—"

"On a Federal charge, Judge. You can't do a thing about it. Just like I told your boss."

"I don't like your tones, Ranger," Holland yelped like a scalded cat. "I am not without friends at the capital and I will get in touch with them."

Waco grinned bleakly. "If you all meaning Senator Flinworthy, he's gone. The good Senator is in Europe taking a long vacation for the good of his health. I don't reckon he'll be back for quite a spell."

The Judge's face showed how well Waco's random shot hit home. "Meaning?"

"Was some talk of investigating certain mining leases that the Senator got all involved in," Waco explained. "What were you saying, Judge?"

Holland turned on his heel and stamped out of the office, followed by the other men. Thorne and the doctor looked with renewed respect at the young Texan, seeing that here was more than just a brave, foolhardy young man with a brace of fast guns to back his play. Here was as smart a man as Allenvale was likely to run across, a man who was unafraid and willing to back any play he made to the limit.

"What was all that about?" Thorne asked.

"Killing an Injun in the reservation is a Federal offence, not local. I've sent and asked Judge Carmody to come for the trial. He's a good man, be likely to strap on a gun himself and help me if I need it."

Before the doctor was finished bandaging up Thorne's leg, a fresh sign of Allenvale's plans showed. Several men from around the town came in and formed a sullen looking group, then one of them spoke.

"We want you to turn Dinty Allenvale loose. You've no witnesses."

"There's one," Waco corrected. "I saw it all and I'm not scared to say so."

"You bunch turn my guts," Thorne growled. There was a change in the man, his face looked stronger, more determined now. "Look at you, a girl is murdered and not one of you dare stand up for the law. Allenvale's men have you scared that bad. It's not loyalty to Allenvale that makes you act like this. Every one of you hates his guts, him and his men. You Sloane," he pointed to a man. "Allenvale's men owe you for leatherwork, they owe Sands there for clothing. You just let them walk all over you and never say a word against them. You're yellow, all of you."

"Never saw you stand up to Allenvale much, neither," a man answered, sullen anger showing on his face.

"That's right, you never did. Things might have been different if I had stood up and done my duty."

The doctor snorted angrily. He eyed the men with cold, hard and contemptuous eyes. "Dan here couldn't do anything when he knew you bunch wouldn't stand by him. He saved the Ranger's life. He's right about you too. Any man who is a man come down to my place in a couple of hours. Now get out of here, fast."

Hawken and Johnny Bren were pitching horseshoes at the back of the store when Magee and Talbot came up. The two gunmen looked around. There was no one in sight so they came in close and Magee said:

"Hawken, you saw Kenny kill that gal, didn't you?"

"It wasn't Kenny, it was Dinty Allenvale," Johnny yelled.

Magee turned and slapped his hand hard across the

youngster's face, spinning him round and knocking him to the ground.

"You stinking, no good rat."

The concentrated fury and hate in the voice brought Magee round, for he could hardly recognise the tones of the storekeeper. Nor could he reconcile the hard, cold-eyed look on the face of the small, fattish man. With a snarl of anger Magee swung his fist at Hawken's head.

For one so slow-looking Hawken acted fast. His head moved, the fist hissing over his shoulder. Then his own fist smashed like a mule-kick right into Magee's stomach, doubling the big gunman over. Hawken's other fist came up, timed just right to catch Magee's jaw as it swung forwards and down. The gunman reared erect and went straight over, landing with legs waving.

Too late Talbot realised what was happening and started to go for his gun. Hawken came in, kicking him scientifically in the stomach and bringing him doubled up, retching violently, to his knees. Hawken closed in, his knee driving up to catch Talbot in the face, smashing him erect and over on to his back.

Magee was on his knees now, fumbling to get his gun out. Hawken went for the big man, catching the gunhand and forcing it up his back. Magee howled as the numbing pain bit into him, then he was spun round and Hawken swung a right with the full weight of his body behind it. The fist caught Magee at the side of the head, knocking the gunman flat again.

"Uncle Henry!" There was open admiration in Johnny's face now as he looked at Hawken's two victims. "Where did you learn to fight like that?"

Hawken turned his attention to the boy, shaking his head slowly as if to clear it. His face looked suddenly old as he patted the boy on the shoulder, "You go on home now, Johnny. Go along, boy."

For a moment Johnny stood there, then turned and hurried off home. Hawken turned and walked back into his store, looking round. This small town had been his home, but he knew it never could be again unless he was willing to rake up his past and do something he did not want to do.

Going into the back room, his small, neat and tidy home, he reached under the bed and pulled out a trunk, opening it.

In the saloon Allenvale looked at his men. The Judge was there, looking pale and worried. Allenvale was in a rage and most of it fell on Holland's head for his inability to release Dinty Allenvale. More than that, Holland refused to take any further interest or part in the matter.

"Two of you boys get out there and warn this bunch that we'll fire every house in town if my boy isn't turned loose," Allenvale ordered.

"I think that is hasty and ill-advised, Mr. Allenvale," Holland put in. "You should wait and see the judge from Tucson."

"A Federal judge?" Allenvale snorted. "I'll get a long way with him."

Magee and Talbot limped in, the others all looked at them. "What happened?" one asked, for they knew the two had been sent to handle Henry Hawken.

"That Ranger was there, Hawken held a gun on us while he worked us over," Magee answered. "They're working together."

"We'll handle Hawken after we've got my boy out," Allenvale answered. "Get going two of you, make sure the folks know what I'm fixing to do."

When the word went out, another deputation gathered in

the marshal's office. The men were all scared-looking although none of them was willing to try open violence to get young Allenvale free. They told Waco the threat Allenvale gave them and waited for his reaction.

"He stays in jail," Waco told them, looking at the men. "One of you go along to the saloon and tell Allenvale that if he is in town in one hour, I'm going to arrest him for intimidating witnesses."

With that the deputation had to be content; they doubted if the Ranger would carry out the threat or if he did would not live to see night fall. One of them took the word to the saloon; the rest of them headed for the doctor's house where a meeting was being held.

The store was silent and unoccupied when Mrs. Bren came in. She went to the rear door, knocked and entered, stopping to look down at the thing which Hawken was holding. Her face was pale, for she was one of the few who knew the secret of Henry D. Hawken. "What are you going to do, Henry?" she asked.

"Help that Ranger."

"You know what that will mean?" Her face showed worry, for she liked and respected the small storekeeper.

"I know. A man can only take so much and I've taken all I mean to. I couldn't look myself in the face again if I let that boy get killed without my helping him. You go to the meeting at the doctor's house and see if you can shake some guts into the men of the town."

The door of the room was thrown open and a frightened looking woman came in. "Becky," she gasped. "It's Johnny. I saw him going along the street with your Ballard; he told my Annie he was going to help the Ranger fight Allenvale."

Hawken straightened up, his eyes blazing, and snapped,

"Get to that meeting and tell them all about that. See if it makes men out of them."

"What about you?"

"The Ranger needs help even more now."

Waco looked at the clock on the office wall and came to his feet. He checked the loads of the matched guns and then started for the door. Thorne levered himself up from the chair, putting weight on his injured leg carefully.

"Where's you going?" Waco asked as the man picked up the shotgun from off his desk.

"With you. This is my town, I reckon I should help maintain the law in it."

"You can't do it," Waco answered.

"Don't you trust me, or want me along?" There was hurt in Thorne's voice.

"Couldn't think of any man I'd rather have along with me," Waco replied. "If you allow your leg will stand it."

"I've got me a Clay Allison crutch," Thorne replied, resting his weight on the shotgun and by holding at the muzzle used it as a walking cane. "Let's go."

"Why sure," Waco agreed. "It's a nice day to get killed."

"You as scared as I am?"

"Yeah, I think so."

In the saloon Allenvale swallowed his drink and looked at the clock. "The hour is up," he said, grinning at the men. "Where's that Ranger?"

"Coming, him and Thorne," one of the men said, from the window. "Want for me to drop them from here?"

"No, let them come."

Judge Holland glanced nervously at Allenvale. Shooting down an unimportant has-been town marshal was one thing; murdering a member of the Arizona Rangers was something entirely different. There would be repercussions which would not be quietened by any amount of bribery or political influence.

"I'm needed at my chambers," he said pompously, reaching for his hat.

"Sit down, Holland," Allenvale snapped. "You've done real well out of me in your time. Now you're running out when there's some real dirty work to be done. Boys, fan out, let them in, then take them."

The gunmen fanned out. Allenvale stood at the bar, watching the batwing doors. All heard the thumping of heels as the two men mounted the sidewalk and came towards the doors.

Then at the side of the room a window broke and a rifle cracked, the bullet sending splinters from the bar by Allenvale's side. Every eye turned towards the window but saw nothing, for the recoil of the Ballard rifle had knocked little Johnny Bren over and out of sight.

The batwings opened and Waco came in, flanked by Thorne, who leaned against the wall and lifted the shotgun across his arm.

"All right, Allenvale," Waco's voice was flat and even. "I'm arresting you for intimidating witnesses. Hand your gun over."

The miner grinned. "You'll have to take it, won't he, boys?"

"Then I'll take it," Waco warned. "If any man draws I'll give it to you, right through the stomach. You know there isn't one of your hired killers fast enough to stop me."

"Mebbe, mebbe not. I'll take my chance on that. These seven boys can take you. Get set boys; it's time we showed this mouthy button who runs this town."

"Yellow as they make 'em!"

The voice came from the side door, all eyes turned that

way. Henry Hawken stood there; yet it was a different Henry Hawken from the man who mildly allowed the gunmen to take goods and never pay for them. He was hard-faced now and at his right side, butt forward, was an ivory butted Colt Dragoon gun, in a well-cared-for holster of a kind they knew too well. A gunfighter's rig.

"What did you say?" Allenvale snarled, looking at the small man.

"I said you were yellow. Those guns there are your guts, take them away and you'd be nothing at all. You're worse than that boy of yours. He killed that girl because she was going to have his child."

"You're a liar!"

Allenvale's hand went under his coat as he spoke. Hawken's right hand twisted palm out, lifting the old Dragoon gun from leather in a fast-done cavalry twistdraw which brought it into line. The roar of the Dragoon shattered the air. Allenvale reared back on his heels, then went down, his gun falling from his hand.

"Get 'em!" Magee yelled, clawing at his gun.

Three guns roared, throwing lead at the gunmen. Waco's left hand fanned off shots so fast they sounded like the rolling of a drum. Then, as three of the hired gunmen joined Magee on the floor, the saloon windows and doors were crowded with armed men.

Waco stood, his gun lined and he snapped, "Drop them."

The remaining gunmen let their guns fall to the floor and the townsmen came crowding in. "What do we do with them, Ranger?" one asked.

"See they pay all they owe you, then let them go," Thorne replied. "I'm obliged to you for arresting Dinty Allenvale, Ranger. I'll take care of things now."

"That's the way it should be," Waco agreed.

The townsmen were gathering round now, looking down

at Allenvale's body, then they realised who had done the shooting.

"Good old Henry," one man yelled. "He got Allenvale. Did you see him shoot?"

The question was to Waco, but Hawken spoke before the Texan could reply. "I was just lucky, I've never used a gun much. Bought this one from a man who came into the store one day."

The townsmen accepted this but Waco knew different. Henry Hawken might have bought the gun from a passing stranger, but he would not have been able to buy a gunbelt which fitted him so well.

"Surely good for you Allenvale wasn't fast with a gun and couldn't get it out from under his coat," Waco remarked to Hawken. "Don't ever try a fool trick like that again."

The crowd looked at the Ranger, then Thorne set them to clearing the bodies out of the saloon. When the crowd was gone, Hawken turned to Waco.

"You know, don't you?"

"I can guess. I've been riding with a gun strapped to my side since I was thirteen. Got to know the signs. You've never worn a glove on your right hand, you've kept in practice with that gun and the belt's well cared for. I reckon I guessed when you didn't come into the saloon last night. Come on, we'd best go and take young Johnny to his mother."

Three days later Waco sat his paint stallion outside the store again. He looked down at Hawken, then ahead to where his partner, Doc Leroy, Judge Carmody and a Federal marshal were escorting young Allenvale into Tucson for trial.

"Thanks again, Waco," Hawken said.

"For what?"

"Helping me cover up who I am. Drango Dune made a lot of enemies and I don't want to have to wear a gun again."

A little girl came from the shop. "Uncle Henry, you never finished that story for us."

Hawken smiled. Once more he was the cherubic little fat man who mildly served in a store. "I never did. Run on in there and I'll come and finish it." He waited until the girl went back, then turned his attention to Waco again. "Drango Dune died the day he killed his friend. I kept the gun and belt and practised with them because I knew that sooner or later we'd have a showdown with Allenvale. But Drango Dune is dead and gone."

"May he rest in peace," Waco answered. "I'd like to hear the end of that story myself. I almost wish I could wait. *Adios.*"

Hawken watched the young Ranger riding off after the other party and for a moment his face was serious. Then turning he walked towards the door of his store. Drango Dune was dead and gone, Henry Hawken had a fairy story to tell the children.

Set One, Catch One

The three plump, sun-reddened businessmen bounced around in a far from comfortable manner in the Wells Fargo coach. The Lordsburg, New Mexico–Tucson, Arizona, trail was neither as well laid out nor as comfortable to travel over as the road from New York to Fairview, New Jersey. Nor was the coach they were now in as comfortable as an eastern carriage. They sat there, lurching and jolting as the coach bounced along, their eastern clothes showing them for what they were, dudes not long in this country. They were a well padded, well dressed bunch and looked like they might be carrying money with them.

The shotgun guard's head appeared at the window of the coach, hanging upside down like a bat. "Mullen's Way Station just ahead, gents," he said. "Change the teams there, be in for about an hour or so, then pull out again and make Tucson just after dark. You can get out and stretch your legs for a piece while we're there."

Alastair Ogden, self-appointed leader of the trio in this venture to the wide open spaces, nodded graciously and the head disappeared again. Ogden did not like the easy familiarity with which the man addressed them all the time. It was not what one expected from a mere employee of a big concern like Wells Fargo. He debated to himself on the advisability of reporting the man, but reached no decision when the coach came to a lurching halt out front of Mullen's Way Station.

For all the name this way station was not an over-impressive place. All it consisted of was one long building which provided a bar, dining-room and a couple of bedrooms, a kitchen and living quarters for the owner and his men. There were a couple of smaller places and along with the large corral where the teams of the coaches milled and waited to be used, formed the whole of Mullen's Way Station.

Ogden and his two friends climbed down from the coach, working their stiff joints and looking round. A tall, burly man came towards them, wearing a frilly bosomed white shirt, string tie, and brown trousers tucked into riding boots. He held out a hand in greeting, his face beaming with delight at the unexpected pleasure.

"Howdy gents, howdy," he said. "Welcome to Honest John Mullen's place. I'm Honest John. Come on in out of the sun."

The other three men followed Mullen into the cool and dim shade of the building. They found themselves in the dining-room which was also the bar, a rough wooden erection presided over by a bald, bored-looking man. Apart from two silent, gun hung men who sat at a table idly playing cards, the place was empty.

"Name your poison, gents, the first is on the house," Mullen boomed. "Allus like to let the customers sample me likker free first, then they knows I'm selling them good stuff."

"Thank you, sir, thank you," Ogden replied, feeling that this bluff, hearty and generous host, while not being an accepted social equal, was worth cultivating. "We are delighted to drink with you. My name is Ogden, these are my friends, Bender and Caldon."

"Most pleasured to make your acquaintance, gents," Honest John shook hands with the men. "Now here's the drinks, put 'em down, gents. It's the first since the last and that's long enough."

Ogden gulped down three fingers of neat whisky in an attempt to emulate the way Honest John ratholed his rye. This brought on a fit of coughing and with tears in his eyes he protested as Honest John slapped him hard on his back.

"Just a mite hard until you get used to it, Mr. Ogden," Mullen warned, then looked at the bardog. "Go get these gents a meal fixed."

The food, when it came, was rough but good, and the three dudes were very hungry. Their meal was a success and their host kept them laughing with a fund of stories. Back East they were pillars of the church and full of civic virtues, strong in their campaigns against sin in all forms. However, away from home they, like many another pious gent, became keenly interested in sin, purely from academic interest, so they could condemn it when they got home. These stories they were now hearing were entertaining, though not the sort one could tell the Reverend Sumpter, back home.

Feeling quite rips, and with a couple of snorts of Old Scalp Lifter under their belts, Ogden and his men thought Honest John a prince among men, a real diamond in the rough. They accepted his invitation to join him at the bar and were just on the point of ordering drinks when the door opened.

The man who came into the room looked old. Straggly long grey hair showed from under his beat-up, dirty hat; the face was also dirty, bristle stubbled and with a few coats of dust on it. He wore a check shirt, the sleeves rolled back and the long red sleeve of an undershirt showing below it; his old blue jeans were stuck into boots and at every step he shed dust. Around his waist was a gunbelt with an old Colt 1860 Army revolver in the holster and a bowie knife strapped at the other side.

"Howdy Honest John," he greeted in a harsh, crackled old voice. "Here I be again. Made my pile out there and come back to show you I can win my bet."

With this the old-timer pulled a pouch from his pocket and tipped it on the bar top. Ogden and his friends gave concerted gasps as they looked down at the glittering pile on the counter before them, for they all suspected that here was real, genuine gold dust gathered from some distant stream.

"So you struck lucky and you aim to try that fool bet again," Honest John growled, looking down at the dust and nuggets on the bar. "Don't you ever learn sense. I've won thirty thousand dollars worth of gold off you and my boys have took near the same. You should know you can't win."

"I can so win," the old-timer bristled aggressively, "and I'm going to prove it."

With this the old-timer turned and stumped across the room to where the two silent, hard-eyed men sat and started to talk with them. His words did not carry to the other men but from his gestures they could see he was getting excited.

"Danged ole fool," Honest John told the dudes. "His name's Wallapai Will, he comes in here every six months or so with a poke of gold and wants to make that fool bet with us."

"What bet is that?" Ogden inquired, wondering how a man could lose so much money on any bet.

"That he can cut the ace of hearts with one cut."

Three faces turned to each other, three minds working out the odds of a man taking a deck of cards and with one single cut picking a selected card. They failed to come anywhere near the correct odds but he knew it ran into thousands to one. Then their eyes went to that pile of gold dust and nuggets on the bar top and they all started to wonder one thing. How could they get their chance at this bet and make some money.

"Is he poor then, apart from this?" Bender inquired, clearing his conscience in advance. "I mean, can he afford to lose like that?"

"Why sure, he's got him a claim there that brings in more than enough money for him. I reckon he could lose this and never even think twice about it."

Wallapai came stamping back to the bar, bristling in fury. "Lookee here, Honest John," he said. "Your boys there tell me they can't bet with me."

"That's right," Honest John answered, turning to face the old-timer. "You never win and we've took enough gold off you."

"Why dednab you for a no good, confounded, interfering coyote," Wallapai was almost spluttering in rage and he turned to the three dudes. "Be that right and fair, gents. That's my gold there, nigh on three thousand dollars worth. If I wants to bet it why should he interfere."

"I suppose Mr. Honest John knows what he's doing," Ogden replied. "If you never win, I mean."

"I ain't won yet, but I surely allows I can this time. He ain't got no right to stop me making the bet."

"You don't make it with me or any of my boys," Honest John warned grimly. "Not if they want to keep on working for me. I'm sick and tired of taking your gold on a fool bet you haven't a chance of winning."

"There's more where that comes form, plenty more." Wallapai turned his bloodshot eyes on the dudes for a moment. "You gents don't work for Honest John. How'd you like—"

"Hold hard, Wallapai, these gents didn't come in here for gambling and I don't want my place turned into a gambling joint."

"Shet up, Honest John," the old-timer snapped back. "These gents are growed men and look like they might like to take a little gamble."

"He might win, gents," Honest John warned.

"We'll confer for a moment," Ogden replied and with his two friends drew away from Honest John and Wallapai. The talked together for a time, apparently not in agreement over something at first. Then they came back. "We feel that we can raise the three thousand to cover the stake. Now, what exactly is the bet?"

"Good!" Wallapai whooped, taking from his pocket a greasy, thick old deck of cards. "Let her rip. I bets I cuts the ace of hearts with just one cut."

"Just one minute." Honest John looked worried, giving the impression that the welfare of his guests was at heart. "The gents would like a new deck used."

The gents certainly did want a new deck but were not quite sure how to ask for one without giving offence. This old-timer looked wild and dangerous enough to be very awkward if crossed, and he was well armed.

Wallapai raised no objections and Honest John took a new deck from the bardog, handing it to Ogden with a request that he break the seal and riffle the cards. With hands that trembled, Ogden took out the new cards and started to shuffle them. Each of his friends gave the cards a thorough shuffle and then the deck was set on the bar top.

"Set your money down to cover mine, gents," Wallapai announced, "then we'll let her rip."

The three men took out their wallets and counted down

a thousand dollars each, leaving them only a few small denomination bills each. They put the money alongside the pile of gold and with the air of a professional gambler Ogden waved a hand to the cards, saying:

"Cut!"

"Hold it," Honest John put in as the old-timer reached for the cards. "I want all this straightened out right off, now. You gents are betting ole Wallapai that he can't cut the ace of hearts with one cut. If he cuts it you lose, if he doesn't you win. That fair enough?"

"Yes, yes, of course it is," Ogden replied impatiently, hands just itching to grab up the gold dust and get back on to the stage again. "Carry on."

Wallapai picked up the cards, holding them firmly in his left hand. He turned them edge up. Round came the bowie knife, ripping into the deck of cards and slicing half-way through them.

"Done it!" the old-timer whooped, tossing the cards on to the bartop and grabbing up the money.

"Wait a minute!" Ogden screeched back. "It's a trick."

"And ye fell for it," Wallapai answered. "I said I'd cut the ace of hearts and cut her I did."

"But—but—, you—you said you'd—This is a swindle," Ogden was all but incoherent with rage.

"Now hold hard a minute, mister." There was a subtle change in Honest John's manner now. It was suddenly menacing, and the two quiet men moved forward. "You made a bet with ole Wallapai here. You said that if he cut the ace of hearts he'd won the bet. Here," sorting through the cards, he tossed the severed ace of hearts in front of them, "that's the ace. Now pay up and shut up."

The three dudes, red-faced and spluttering, stared at the cards, then at the men. Slowly it dawned on them that they were being threatened, for all the easy benevolence had drained from Honest John now, leaving a hard-faced man. Somehow Wallapai looked years younger too, his face mocking and a sneer on his lips. The two silent, hard-faced men lounged near at hand: they watched everything with solid, dispassionate eyes, hands on the butts of their guns.

It was at this moment that the guard looked inside and told Ogden's party the coach was ready to move. He could guess what had happened here, but was powerless to make any objection. The bar was not Wells Fargo property and the company had no control over it. The dudes would complain to the company but would receive no comfort there; Mullen's Way Station was the only place a relay point could be placed in that area and under the lease, Mullen could run his bar any way he wanted. Wells Fargo might not approve of having their customers robbed but there was nothing they could do about it officially.

Muttering threats of revenge the three dudes walked from the bar and out in the sun once more. They climbed into the coach, bitterness etched on their faces and a desire for revenge in their hearts.

Mullen watched the coach moving out from his side window, and he grinned at the other men. Wallapai was washing his face in the corner. He turned round, rubbing it with a towel; no longer did he look old, he was a middle-aged man with a thin, intelligent face.

"Damned suckers," he said. "You certainly know how to pick them, John."

"Sure, with their sort you have to make them feel they're real bloods before they'll bite. There won't be another stage for three days so we can take it easy."

"I hold here four aces." Doc Leroy held the four cards so Captain Mosehan could see them. "Now I place them on top of the deck. Like so. Take the top ace off and put it on the bottom of the deck, the second ace and put it quarter way down and the third three-quarters of the way down. Leaving one ace on top," Doc showed the ace on top of the deck and the one at the bottom. "All four now being separated, I place the deck on the desk and strike it once, so!" Doc struck the deck hard with the flat of his hand. "Then cut the deck like this," he made a fast cut, then fanned the deck out, "to find in the middle one, two, three, four little aces all together."

Mosehan laughed, holding out his hand for the deck and checking through it but finding only the four aces. "All right, I give it up. How do you do it? I thought you'd palmed the middle two aces somehow and held them out, then put them on top when you slapped the deck."

Doc took the four aces up and two other cards, then placing the two cards behind the second ace so that they did not show, he folded the cards and laid them on top of the deck.

"One ace on the bottom," he slid the top card off, showing the ace and put it on the bottom. "One ace in the middle," this time it was not an ace which went from the top of the deck into the middle. "One lower down," again it was not an ace. "One ace left on top. Only there are three aces on top, not one. Cut the cards and in the middle of the deck you have four aces."

Mosehan laughed, watching Doc riffle the cards with tapering, almost boneless-looking hands. Doc was a tall, slim young man with a studious, pallid face but it was a tan-resisting pallor, not weakness. He was slender in build but there was a whipcord strength in his wiry frame. Doc was a cowhand, a good one; any man who trailed cattle for the edge trail crews was a tophand. Doc not only trailed for them but also handled the tough doctoring chores, for he'd started at medical school although he gave it up before he qualified. His reputation as a setter of bones and remover of bullets was known throughout the West. At least three babies were in this world due to his efforts and one man owed his life to Doc's removal of his appendix with the highly technical, surgical instrument, a bowie knife.

With the end of the trail drives, the great, interstate journeys from Texas to Kansas, Doc joined Ole Devil Hardin, riding as Waco's pard in the floating outfit of the OD Connected. Then when Waco was wounded he stayed with him until he recovered; it was Doc's medical skill which saved Waco's life. They'd been taken on at the Hashknife where Mosehan had been manager, to make enough money to head back to Texas. When Mosehan formed the Rangers he brought them with him: he did not regret the decision, for they were amongst his best men.

Watching the slim young man in the range coat and the jacket with its right side stitched back to leave clear the ivory butt of his Colt Civilian Peacemaker, Mosehan was pleased. Doc was waiting to be sent out on a local chore, having just watched his pard, Waco, ride out for Allenvale.

The long, fast-moving fingers split the cards in the middle and married them together with a fast rifflestack; then he cut the cards twice or appeared to be cutting them, but the same cards remained on the bottom all the time.

"You're wasting your time in the Rangers," Mosehan remarked dryly as Doc went on to deal four hands of cards out. Fetching from the bottom a full house for himself and doing it without Mosehan, no mean gambler himself, catching him at it. "You ought to be on a sternwheeler going up and down the Big Muddy."

"Couldn't stand all that water," Doc replied.

There was a knock at the door and the young man who handled the Rangers' paper and office work looked in.

"Mr. Hume, from Wells Fargo, and three gents to see you, Cap'n Mosehan."

"Show 'em in, Jeb. Show 'em in," Mosehan replied, signing Doc to stay.

A tall, good-looking, wide shouldered man wearing range clothes came into the office, followed by Ogden and his party. Jim Hume was one of Wells Fargo's top men, a special investigator with a reputation for bringing in his man. He was an old friend of Mosehan and co-operated with the Rangers on the occasions when their line of duty came together.

"I brought these three gentlemen to see you, Bert," he said.

"It's an outrage, sir. A deliberate outrage." Ogden stepped by Hume, his face working angrily. "I demand action. I demand that our money is recovered. We've been robbed and swindled."

"How?" Mosehan glanced at Jim Hume but could read nothing on his face.

"How?" It was Bender now giving vent to his outraged feelings. "How! By a dirty trick. That old prospector said he would cut the ace of hearts—"

"Didn't he do it?" Mosehan heard Doc's choked down gurgle of amusement and saw the ghost of a smile on Hume's face.

"He cut it all right," Ogden answered. "Or he didn't cut it, he used a knife—"

"But we thought he meant to cut the cards, not use a knife." Ogden was beginning to see his position and was wondering how he could explain his own actions in anything like a creditable light. He couldn't come right out and say he'd planned to make the bet against a foolish old man who should not have had a chance. He could also see that the three men in the room were not exactly unaware of the trick.

"What do you want me to do, gents?" Mosehan asked.

"Unless you can prove a definite swindle I can't move. You made a legal bet; in Arizona gambling is legal and I can't arrest him just for cutting cards with you."

"Bah!" Ogden's angry snort sounded more like the bleating of a sheep stuck with a pitchfork. "Wells Fargo can't help us, the county sheriff says the way station is over the county line and he can't do a thing. Now you say you can't help."

"What did you expect me to be able to do?" Mosehan growled. "You name it and we'll try and do it."

There the three dudes had it; they could tell Mosehan what they wanted doing and he would get it done. All they had to do was put some light on their own motives for making the bet and they might be able to make a complaint. They turned and headed for the door muttering threats about seeing the governor.

Mosehan watched them go, his face thoughtful: he knew their type all too well. Fresh out from the East, they thought every man they met in the West was an illiterate, slow-witted yokel ripe for plucking. When they learned, too late, that the stupid yokel was the one who'd done the plucking they screamed to high heaven. Worse, they reported the incident, highly coloured on their side, to the Eastern Press and stories of Western lawlessness ranged high amongst the stories the Eastern papers printed.

"There's not much I can do about it, gents, but I'll try and get your money back for you."

With that the three dudes had to be satisfied. They left the office and were spared the humiliation of seeing Doc Leroy howling in laughter at the thought of anyone falling for the old ace cutting game in this day and age.

"Lordy, Lord," he said, "I surely thought the old ace cutting game went out with the cap and ball guns."

"Looks like it came back again," Mosehan answered.

"Why'd you come across with them, Jim. You know we can't do anything about it."

"Unless you can prove definite fraud," Hume replied. "Then both you and Wells Fargo can make a move. We've been getting complaints from the Mullen's Way Station for a spell now but we can't tie them down with anything. A man won't go into court and admit he made a fool of himself. Anyways, you can't arrest a man for making a bet."

"We might be able to get evidence," Mosehan said thoughtfully. "Then we can move in. We need a plant, a man who can be took."

Doc smiled; he knew this boss of his very well. "When do I start?" he asked.

Mullen got a shock when a stagecoach came rumbling into the way station on the afternoon two days after the successful rooking of the three dudes. He strolled down to the corral where the teams were being changed, noting that a tall stranger was riding shotgun. A man who looked vaguely familiar and also looked handy with the staghorn butted gun tied low at his left side.

"What's all this?" he asked the driver.

"Howdy John," the driver replied, jerking his thumb to a slim young man who was climbing down from the coach. "Rich young dude in a hurry to get East again. He hired this coach special to run him to Lordsburg."

Mullen studied the young man, noting the pallid face but paying more attention to the high hat. It was very costly beaver from the look of it and the travelling cloak the young man wore was black, lined with red silk. It covered most of his clothes but Honest John could see a white silk shirt, a costly cravat and a diamond stick pin which made his eyes gleam avariciously.

"Howdy sir, allow me to introduce myself." Mullen advanced, hand held out. "I'm Honest John Mullen, owner of the way station here. If you'd care to step into my place for a meal while the teams are being changed."

"Why most certainly, sir, I could eat something," the voice was a cultured deep south drawl.

Doc followed Honest John into the bar, glanced at the two hard-faced men who sat watching him, then went to the bar and accepted a glass of whisky on the house. He took his place at the table, throwing the cloak back slightly but making sure the right side of his suit could not be seen. Outside, he knew Mosehan would be watching from the window of the coach, where he'd been hidden, and Jim Hume also was getting ready to move in.

Honest John gave the order for the food and his bardog left, hurrying to one of the small side buildings to tell Wallapai he would be needed. The thin man gave an angry curse, he'd shaved this morning, not expecting another stage. That gave him only one alternative. He rummaged through the box he pulled from under the bed and brought out a well-made straggly false beard.

Doc enjoyed the meal and was rather pleased when the door opened to admit the "old sourdough prospector." A keen student of the art of taking suckers, Doc had to admit it was all well done. In fact, if he did not know about this set-up he might even have been fooled by Wallapai himself.

Rising, he sauntered to the bar and was treated to the same sort of build-up the other victims were given. He glanced at the "gold," seeing it was only fools' gold, worthless quartz, but gave the impression he was taken in.

When the prospector failed to get his bet with Honest John's two men and came back to the bar, Doc gave a creditable performance as the sucker who wanted to make some extra money fast.

"How about you, stranger. You wanting to take a chance?" Wallapai asked.

"I wouldn't mind," Doc replied. "Is that real gold? I've never seen any like this before, in its raw state."

"Real gold?" Wallapai's face showed anger. "Of course it's real gold. I just come in from my gold claim with it."

Mullen gave his agreement that it was real gold and that Wallapai went into the hills to prospect for it. He acted grudgingly, giving the impression that he did not want any betting in his place. The more determined he was to stop it, the more insistent Doc became.

"All right," Mullen placed two decks of cards on the table. "If you're all set to make the bet use one of those two decks, then you'll know you've had a square deal."

"It's a pity you've only got two thousand in gold there," Doc remarked, taking a bulging notecase from his inside pocket. "I'd go up to five thousand that he can't cut the ace."

There was an awkward silence for a time; Mullen and Wallapai always tried to guess how much the sucker would go for and put that much gold out. Now they could see they'd gone under. However, they had a plan arranged for such an emergency.

"Honest John, I've got me three thousand dollars in your safe there," the "prospector" said. "Git her out, this is my lucky day."

The money was counted out and matched Doc's own pile on the counter. Doc took up the cards, extracted them from the box and gave them a casual, awkward overhand stack. The others looked at each other; from the way he handled cards this dude was the veriest beginner.

Laying the cards on the bar top Doc stepped back, his left hand going to the fastening of the cloak as he said, "Cut!"

With a grin Wallapai took up the cards, holding them

edge up and brought out his bowie knife, slashing down deep into the deck. He dropped the cards on the bar and reached for the money.

"Hold hard, friend. You didn't cut the ace of hearts."

There was a different note in the drawl now; Mullen did not turn to look at the young man, but took up the cards and thumbed through them, looking for the ace of hearts. He went through the deck without finding the card and his face deepened into a scowl as he started through again.

"It's here."

Mullen turned. The slim young man's cloak had slid from his shoulders and lay on the floor. He wore a brown suit under it, the right side of the jacket pinned back. Around his waist was a handcarved buscadero gunbelt and in the low tied, gunfighter's holster a white handled gun. But it was at his right hand that Mullen stared; one moment the hand was empty, then with a snap of his fingers the young man produced and tossed the ace of hearts down.

"Get him, boys!" Mullen roared, hand dropping down towards his waistband.

Doc's hand made a fast flicker, the gun appearing with the sight defying speed of a master. He threw one shot into the gunman who was first to make his move, staggering him backwards across the room.

At the same moment the door was kicked open, and Mosehan and Hume came in fast, their guns out. Wallapai was throwing down on Doc when Hume fired once, the bullet smashing into his leg and dropping Wallapai to the floor. The other men threw up their hands.

"That'll finish you, John," Hume warned. "We have proof of fraud now. We saw your 'prospector' coming out of the hills, only it was the hut back there. I reckon we'll find his make-up bit hidden in there."

Doc looked thoughtful; a good lawyer might get Mullen

out of it even now: he could play on the provocational way in which Mullen was trapped and might get the man free. But good lawyers were hard to come by and their services very expensive. Doc knew there was more money in the safe, money they could not touch: legally.

He attended to Wallapai's leg; the other shot man was dead before he could do a thing for him. Then as they were waiting for the stage he took up the second deck of cards and fanned them out, holding them face down.

"Here, John, take one," he said.

Mullen was about to snarl a refusal, then he shrugged. He had been caught out fairly and held little or no grudge against the young Ranger. He could even admire the skill which palmed out the ace while giving that misleading and casually amateurish overhand stack of the cards.

Reaching out he took a card, at least, he thought he chose a card but the nine of spades he showed to the others was forced on him by Doc.

"Put her back and riffle them well," Doc said.

With the cards well mixed Doc took them and started to turn them over, counting as he did. The nine of spades fell on the fifteenth card but Doc carried on and at the twenty-third, pushing it forward but not turning it he said, "The next card I turn over will be the one you picked out."

"Will it?" Mullen asked, glancing down at where he could see the corner of the chosen nine.

"I'd surely bet on it," Doc replied.

At the word bet Mullen looked eager. He was thinking along the same lines as Doc: a good lawyer would be worth money if he could get them off this charge, for it could go hard on them. They all had records with the Pinkerton Agency for this sort of swindle. Pinkertons would be only too pleased to serve the interests of justice, and get some good publicity for themselves, by producing this record in court.

"I got me two thousand dollars more in the safe," he said. "I'll get that and bet it."

"Done," Doc agreed.

"You know what you're doing, boy?" Mosehan asked, temporarily forgetting that Doc was not gambling with his own money.

"Why sure, I know."

Hume escorted the handcuffed Mullen to the safe as a precaution against tricks. However it was money and money only Mullen brought out and took back to count down against Doc's two thousand.

"I'll take fifty of that," Mosehan remarked, not quite sure what Doc was up to. "If you like."

"I'll have fifty myself," Jim Hume agreed.

All eyes were on the top card of the deck, waiting for Doc's discomfiture when he turned it. His other hand reached out, extracted the nine of spades from where it lay and turned it over.

"But you told us—" Mullen began, then his mouth dropped open and he gave a strangled croak of, "You tricked us."

"Why sure, now you know how it feels," Doc replied. He scooped up the money, pushing the large heap towards Jim Hume. "You might be able to find some of the folks they swindled and pay them back."

Hardie nodded, then watched Doc scoop up the ten dollar bills which Hume and Mosehan had put down in the bet. Doc took out his notecase and slipped them in.

"Hey, that's my money, mine and Jim's," Mosehan objected.

"And you just lost it," Doc replied. "I always told you gambling'd be your ruin, Cap'n Bert."

• • •

It was the day after Doc's return from a hurried ride to Allenvale to help Waco out. The two young men were being sent out on another assignment and Doc was just going to tell Mosehan and Waco, who were in the office, that the horses were ready.

He opened the door and heard something which made him stay quiet. Mosehan and Waco were at the desk, the Captain holding part of a deck of cards, the other part on the table before him.

"All right then, boy, you're betting your pay cheque against my seventy dollars that the next card I turn over isn't the one you picked?"

"Why sure," Waco agreed, laying his pay cheque on the table alongside the money Mosehan had placed there. With the same move he scooped up the cards from the desk and put them in his pocket. "Turn ahead, Cap'n."

Mosehan heard Doc's laugh and turned, scowling. Waco put the money and his pay cheque into his pocket, took his hat up and headed for the door.

"Did you teach him that damned trick, Doc?" Mosehan asked.

"Why no, I'll confess I didn't," Doc answered. "See, Waco was the one who taught it to me."

Before the speechless Captain of Rangers could say another word the door shut. Before he had time to get to his feet and go after the two jovial tricksters he heard hooves and knew they were already on their way. He went back to his desk, sat down and shook his head.

"My mammy told me there'd be days like this," he said.

Buffalo Soldier

"What're you doing in here, nigger?"

The War between the States was long over and the freed slaves were leaving their homes, spreading out across the land in search of work. Many of them, full of pipedreams, headed north, out of the cottonlands of the deep south, into the land of promise. There they expected to be treated as equals and to find a land flowing with milk and honey. North to the land of the people who fought the War to give them freedom. This migration caused many people to wonder as to the wisdom of their actions. It was fine and patriotic to talk about all men being free and the rights of man, but it was only the people who did not need to worry about the Negroes taking their work who talked that way. The others, the poor class who did the fighting held no brief for or against slavery. Few of them would have considered the conditions the average slave worked under as being worse than their own. It was this poorer class who saw the influx and felt the true effect of this cheap labour which moved in on them.

The problem that the freed slaves caused was already being felt in New York and the repercussions were echoing in the tiny frontier hamlet of Orejano, Arizona.

Sam Bone halted on his way back to the bar of the only saloon in Orejano. His black face showed no expression as he turned to see who was speaking, for he was accepted here amongst the free and easy white men of the frontier as their social equal. The accents of the speaker were not, as a chance stranger might have expected, the deep southern drawl. Rather they were the harsh tones of New York and not the better part of New York at that.

Turning, Sam Bone saw what he feared and felt sickness in the pit of his stomach. The speaker was a tall, darkly handsome young man wearing the uniform of a trooper in the United States Cavalry, and would be part of that detachment which was even now setting up a temporary camp outside town. By his side stood a second, not so tall, or so handsome soldier, mirroring the first's truculence.

Bone turned back towards the bar as the two came from the sidetable where they'd been seated. He saw his friend, the old bardog, polishing a glass with a rag that might have been new about the time of the first battle of Bull Run, and taking everything in.

"Vin here asked you a question, nigger," the second young man said.

"Just came in for a drink, friend," Sam answered.

"Did you now?" The one called Vin teetered forward, a half empty whisky bottle in his hand. "Then you can just drag on out again. We don't let no nigger drink in the same place as us. Do we, Jocko?"

"Thought you Yankees made all men free?" the old bardog asked as he dropped a hand under the bar counter towards the butt of his sawed-off ten gauge.

Vin Bartelmo, product of the Bowery, even then one of the toughest suburbs of New York, slouched forward and thrust his face over the bar, looking down at the old-timer.

"You shut your face, old man, or I'll shut it with a boot.

Sure we set them lousy niggers free, but now they're coming north and taking all the work. Folks won't take on
white men when they can get niggers and they'll let white
men off to take on niggers. That's all they're good for,
taking white men's work."

"Not me, friend," Sam Bone spoke gently, trying to
steer off the anger of the young soldier before there was
serious trouble. "I don't need no more work, got more than
enough of my own."

"Yeah?" Bartelmo sneered back, looking at his friend
and fellow New Yorker, Jocko Davies. "I bet it's work
some white man would have been doing if you hadn't took
it away from him."

Sam Bone couldn't argue about that at all, for he was
doing a white man's work. It was a leatherwork shop left to
him by the man who had brought him west as a servant,
attendant and friend, the man who had been reared with
him on a plantation in Georgia: the man who'd been both
master and good friend.

However, Sam wanted no trouble with these two soldiers, for he knew the Army would always side with their
own kind against any civilian. In the deep south the Army
might once have enforced a strictly "if he's black he's
right" policy, but not out in Arizona and at this time. He
knew that the bardog would back up his play to the hilt but
that would only get the old-timer into bad trouble.

"If you feels that strong about it, white boy, I'll go," he
said.

Even as Sam turned from the bar and walked away,
Bartelmo put a foot in his back and shoved hard. Sam
Bone staggered forward, hitting a table and hanging on to
it to stop himself crashing to the floor. His face showed
some anger as he turned.

"Don't you go abusing this coon no more, soldier boy,"

he warned, his voice brittle with anger. "I was a soldier long 'fore you was borned."

Bartelmo smashed the bottle against the bar, his face twisted into a savage sneer as he moved forward. Outside he heard horses stop and the thump of heels as two men came to the batwing doors. He thought they would be other members of his troop coming for a drink. This would serve to show the others how the tough men of New York handled things. He moved in with the bottle held, its cruel, jagged ends aiming to rip into the black face.

The batwings swung open and two tall, Texas men entered. Texas men, or their range clothes and their star decorated Justin boots lied. They were a handy-looking pair, one slightly taller, wide of shoulder, lean of waist and handsome, wearing a buscadero gunbelt and a matched pair of staghorn-butted Colt guns in the carefully placed holsters. The second was slim, pallid and studious-looking, though there was a whipcord hardiness about him that did not go with the pallor. He, like his friend, wore range clothes except that he wore a brown coat, the right side stitched back to leave clear the ivory butt of his low holstered Colt Civilian Peacemaker.

For an instant they halted, taking in the scene. Then the taller moved forward with hands just brushing the butts of his matched guns. Halting between Bone and the drunken soldier he snapped:

"I'm a Ranger. Put down that bottle. Right now."

Bartelmo teetered on his heels, looking at the tall young Texan, then he swung the bottle up like it was a meat axe meaning to smash the jagged ends down at this rash stranger who'd come between him and his fun.

The Texan's right hand dipped faster than the eye could follow, the bar light glinted dully on the five-and-a-half inch barrel of the Artillery Peacemaker in his palm and flame tore from the muzzle. The bottle exploded and Bartelmo yelled as chips of glass showered on him, stinging his face. The yell of pain ended abruptly as the Texan's gun whirled back to leather in a smooth move which ended with the same hand, now a fist, sinking into Bartelmo's Old Scalplifter filled belly. With a grunt of pure agony the soldier doubled forward, then a hand gripped his collar and heaved. Bartelmo shot by the Texan and landed on hands and knees at the feet of the second of that reckless breed.

Filled full of whisky and misguided loyalty to his friend, Davies swung a blow at the tall Texan who'd dealt so roughly with Bartelmo. It was a good punch but just seemed to melt in thin air as the Texan struck back. Hitting with the same speed as he'd drawn his gun, the Texan got a lot of weight behind his punch; Davies went backwards across the room, smashed into the bar and hung there for a moment, then slid down with a blissful expression on his face.

Bartelmo got to his knees, holding his stomach and snarling in pained anger as he fumbled to get the gun out of his holster. The second Texan looked down with mild benevolence. Studious-looking or not he could move with a speed that was at least equal to his fast-moving friend's. His boneless-looking hand dipped and the Colt came out, lifting then coming down with force and precision right behind the soldier's ear, dropping him back to the ground again.

"Nice moving gents," the bartender said delightedly. "Belly up and have something on the house."

The taller of the pair grinned, the grin making him look even more boyish than ever, but the blue eyes were not young; they were eyes that met a man's yet showed little of what the Texas boy was thinking.

"Root beer then, cold as you've got, a meal and some information."

The bardog's eyes grew frosty and wolf cautious. He'd

heard the young man describe himself as an Arizona Ranger and it did not pay a man to answer too many questions.

"Beer's as cold as I can git it," he answered. "I can fix you up with a meal if you've got time to wait for me to cook it. But information is something I'm long done out of."

"We'll take the first two then, friend." The other man joined his partner at the bar. "I can't take any more of Waco's cooking and mine's even worse."

For a moment the bardog studied the men, taking in the spread of the man called Waco's shoulders and the lean lithe form of the other. That one name meant something to him.

"Waco, huh?" he asked, relaxing slightly. "You'll be Doc Leroy then?"

"Right as the off side of a hoss, Colonel," Waco replied. "We're here looking to meet a gent called Sam Bone."

Before another word could be said the batwings opened and a tall, handsome young Lieutenant followed by a short, tough-looking corporal entered. They stopped at the door, looking down at the two recumbent figures on the floor. The officer frowned as his eyes went to the group at the bar.

"What's all this?" he asked grimly.

"They you'rn?" Waco answered, meeting the officer's eyes without flinching. "You should keep them muzzled mister. Took on too much bravemaker, got rough, got all tuckered out and laid them down to sleep."

"Though I can't see anyone wanting their souls to keep," Doc Leroy went on. "I reckon you'll be Mr. Beaulieu of the Seventh?"

"I am."

"Cap'n Mosehan of the Arizona Rangers sent us down here to team up with you."

"Then it would have been more correct to report to your officer instead of making for the first saloon," Beaulieu snapped. He was young and not long out of West Point, but he did not intend to allow these two civilians, even if they were members of the Arizona Rangers, to make a fool of him. He meant to show them from the very start that this was an Army patrol and would be run as such.

"Mister," Waco's voice was cold and unfriendly. "The only officer we've got was at Tucson last herd count, he isn't here."

"And we came in here to ask about the scout who'll be coming with us," Doc put in, attempting to stop conflict.

To hide his confusion, Beaulieu turned and ordered the corporal to take the two unconscious men out and souse them in the water trough, then get them back to the camp lines. The corporal took hold of Bartelmo's collar, dragged him to where Davies lay, then with one collar in each hand hauled them out through the door. Beaulieu watched them go, then turned and gave his full attention to the two Rangers.

"And did you find that scout?"

"Never had a chance, you came in afore the gent behind the bar could answer our question," Waco replied. "Do you know anybody called Sam Bone?"

The bartender and the Negro started laughing, then Bone pointed a black finger at his chest. "I'm Sam Bone, suh. At least I is one Sam Bone, there might be more of us. I dunno, ain't only met but me."

"You?" Beaulieu's face showed his surprise; he came from Boston and the only Negroes he'd ever seen were house servants. "Are you the scout?"

"Why wouldn't he be, mister?" Waco asked.

Beaulieu flushed red, realizing that he was getting off on the wrong foot with the men he would have to rely on so much in the next few days. "Cap'n Daniels said you took him out after the Apache Kid last year. He speaks highly of you, Mr. Bone."

"We never caught the Kid, though it weren't for looking."

"Don't let that fret you none, Sam," Doc answered. "The pick of the Arizona Rangers couldn't catch him either, could we, Waco?"

"Some pick!" Beaulieu snorted, then grinned at the other two. He was one of the new officers of the 7th Cavalry. The hard drinking, hard fighting, hard headed men who rode under Custer were for the most part no longer with the regiment. The ones who survived Custer's folly at the Little Bighorn were for the most part posted to other regiments. They would never have taken the word or acted human with a pair of civilians. He was sensible enough to know that he was not trained for the sort of work they were going to undertake. These two men knew the country, knew the people who lived in it. If he treated them as human beings they would do the same for him and help him all they could. He would get nowhere by flouting his West Point superiority with these two reckless sons of the saddle; they respected a man for what he was, not who he was.

"Do you know the border well, Sam?" he asked.

"He knows it better'n most, soldier boy," the bardog growled. "Ole Sam here's the best scout the Army's got and I don't bar Tom Horn nor Seiber from your count."

This news relieved Beaulieu, for the task he was going out on was not easy. The adjutant of the Seventh made that quite clear when briefing Beaulieu for the assignment. He made one point clear beyond all others. On no account must the patrol cross the International Line into Mexico. They were to go out and patrol in the hope of catching the notorious bandido, Augustine Chacon, but they must not go into Mexico under any circumstances.

Two other young Lieutenants of the Seventh had already come to grief on such an assignment, for the Mexican Government raised a mighty howl at what they termed an armed invasion of their territory.

To prevent this occurring with more serious results, Beaulieu was taking a civilian scout who knew the border and two Arizona Rangers. Waco and Doc had a very special part to play if they should manage to run across Chacon and cut him off from his men. Under a gentleman's agreement between Captain Mosehan and Don Emilo Kosterliski, the Commander of the Guardia Rurale, members of either organisation could disregard the border when in the pursuit of one of their own nationals who slipped across in the hope of gaining immunity. This, however, was a purely unofficial arrangement and did not apply to Chacon, who was a Mexican citizen. But Kosterliski had told Mosehan he would close both eyes to any attempt to take the murdering bandido, even if the said taking was done in Mexico.

That was what brought Waco and Doc to Orejano, to patrol with the Army; giving them a fighting force to match against Chacon's murderous gang. Then if Chacon got back over the border, to bring him in, dead or alive.

"When can we start?" Beaulieu asked.

"We've got us the scout and the soldiers." Waco ignored Beaulieu, winking at Doc. "So after ole granpappy here gets his tired old hide into the kitchen and raises us a meal we'll be all set to go."

The bardog growled something about the young folks of today having no respect for age or wisdom; spat into the spitoon across the room and walked out into the kitchen. Beaulieu stepped out of the saloon and told his corporal, who was just getting Bartelmo and Davies on to their feet. The young officer gave orders for camp to be broken and the troop ready to move out; then he returned and sat with Waco and Doc. It came as something of a surprise to him that these two southerners would allow Sam Bone to sit at their table with them, for he thought that all men of the deep south treated Negroes like dirt, whipping or shooting them at the slightest excuse. He was beginning to realise that the southern man knew more, far more, about Negroes than himself.

"You know our mission, of course?" he asked.

"Sure," Waco agreed. "Chacon is supposed to be across the border. That means he most likely isn't. But if he is, then Cap'n Mosehan thinks he'll head for the border up this way, between here and Sasabe on the California line. That's why we are patrolling out that way."

"One thing, mister," Doc warned. "We might or might not run into Chacon or one of the other Mexican gangs. If we run into Chacon don't you go selling him short. He'll likely have up to fifty men riding with him against your troop of twenty and us three. Happen he gets the idea we're hunting him, ole *Peludo*'ll just as likely come looking for us."

"He's only a Mexican," Beaulieu scoffed.

"And Sitting Bull was only an Indian."

Beaulieu's face flushed deep red. Any mention of the disaster which befell the 7th Cavalry at the Little Bighorn rankled amongst the officers of the regiment, who were trying to live it down.

"So?"

"Don't you go swell up and bust, not while I'm eating," Doc's grin robbed the words of their sting. "I was born on the border of Texas and all my life I've known Mexicans. They can count real good and likewise know that odds of two or three to one is good medicine. Specially from ambush and with the chance of getting some free Cavalry Peacemakers out of the deal."

Once more Beaulieu's inborn sensibility came to his aid and he looked at the two with a friendly smile. He could see a difference in their attitude towards him even now and knew they would do all they could for him.

"All right, I'll put myself in your hands; then when the

Court Martial convenes I'll say I was led astray by evil companions and they'll go light on me."

After the meal Waco and Doc rode with Beaulieu to the Army camp. The patrol were going to travel light and would be leaving the tents here under guard until they returned. The troopers were waiting by their horses, Bartelmo and Davies looking worse for wear along with the others. They watched the Texans with hate-filled eyes and then turned their attention to where Sam Bone came riding up afork a mule that looked as old as sin and even more wicked.

"Look there, that nigger's riding scout for us," Bartelmo hissed in a voice which carried all along the line.

"Yeah," Davies agreed, his voice also carrying. "I bets he took that on when there was a white man who could have done it."

Waco hurled the big paint stallion back along the line and brought it to a dust raising halt before the two startled troopers as they struggled to control their shying horses. He waited until the two got their horses under control then leaned forward, thrusting his face towards the men: his voice was vibrant with anger as he said:

"Now listen to me, soldier. I'm saying this but once, so you lay back your ears and listen real good. Leave Sam Bone be. He's doing a chore that not many men would want to handle, not living down here on the border. Get this into your damned, hawgstupid Yankee head. Ole Sam, he lives down here in Orejano. If Chacon gets to know he's riding scout against him, Sam's life won't be worth a Yankee's word to an Injun. And soldier, that's not worth much. Sam's not like you, he doesn't have a regiment of cavalry round to protect him all the time."

Bartelmo looked back, then his eyes dropped and he snarled. "I won't forget what you did to me in that saloon."

"Happen you won't," Waco answered. "But remember this. I could just as easy put the bullet into your fool head. Next time I have to draw on you I'll do just that and think nothing of it."

The soldier snarled under his breath but kept his mouth shut until Waco turned the paint and rode back to the head of the line where Beaulieu sat watching. Bartelmo's hand dropped, unfastened the revolver holster and curled round the butt of his gun.

Corporal Machie slammed his horse forward, barking out, "Take your hand off that gun, you damned fool. Look there."

Bartelmo looked and suddenly his stomach went cold: he could see that he was very close to an early grave. Doc Leroy was sitting afork his black horse; in his hands, its bore looking like the mouth of a cannon, was a Winchester Centennial rifle. While it was actually only .45.75 calibre the gun looked far larger when it was pointed in one's stomach at that range.

"Happen you're tired of life in the Seventh, you just lift the gun clear," Doc said cheerfully. "I don't reckon the regiment will fold up and fade away without you along."

Bartelmo let loose of the gun; he could see the eyes of the other troopers on him, for he was known amongst the other recruits who formed his patrol as being a hardcase. They would begin to wonder if he was so hard after all.

Beaulieu watched all this with worried eyes: it was his first assignment on his own and he could see there was going to be trouble unless he kept a firm check on Bartelmo. For a moment he thought of leaving the soldier behind but knew that would be foolish. Bartelmo was not to be trusted with movable property and would probably sell the tents. There was only one thing to do, take him along and watch him all the time.

Raising his hand, the young Lieutenant gave the order to march out.

For three days the patrol moved through the arid border country, travelling slowly and checking every likely spot for sign of passing Mexican bandits. They found no new sign at all but it made good training for Beaulieu. The Apache wars were over but the conditions they worked under now were almost the same. There was a need for constant vigilance and the men were alert. The first day they'd been inclined to take things easy, but that night around the fire Waco had told them how Chacon and other Mexican bandits treated gringo prisoners. He warned them that the Mexican was an expert at ambush and would lay the patrol given a chance. In graphic words he warned them of the danger and they believed him, knowing that he was telling the truth.

From that time they rode cautiously and acted as if they were working against Apaches. Of all the soldiers only Machie was a veteran; he'd seen service with the Seventh against Apaches and was with Reno's troops at the Little Bighorn. He, with the help of Sam Bone and the Rangers, taught his men the secrets of desert survival and most of them learned well.

Yet over all the patrol was the brooding troublecausing of Bartelmo and his friend. Davies was a mere sycophant, following Bartelmo's lead, and they worked at turning the others against Sam Bone and the two Texans. They did it on the sly, for neither was willing to tangle with Waco again. For the most part they did not have much success at turning the country boys against Sam Bone. The southern recruits knew Negroes and accepted Sam as a man doing a difficult job. The northern recruits, coming from country villages, rarely, if ever, saw Negroes and treated Sam as an equal without thinking about it. Just a few, city bred like Bartelmo, were willing to follow him and even they would not argue against that tall, slow talking but fast moving Texan.

On the third night Bartelmo watched Sam Bone talking with some of the recruits round one of the fires. He nudged Davies and rose, walking across, listening to the laughter as Sam told the soldiers some story. Bartelmo pushed through and stood, looking down at Sam Bone.

"Hey, nigger, what did you do in the War while us white folks was fighting to set you free?"

"Why I fought too."

"You fought?"

"I sure did, white boy. I fought and I fought and I fought. But it weren't no use at all. They got me in the Army in the end."

There was a roar of laughter from the men round the fire at this, the laughter bringing Bartelmo's temper to an uncontrollable pitch and he snarled, "Get up, nigger, I'm going to kick your face in."

Waco came to his feet in a lithe bound, coming in between Bartelmo and Sam Bone, his soft easy drawl bringing the other man to a halt.

"Soldier, you've said more than enough. Get yourself back to your fire or I'll finish what I started in Orejano."

Machie was also on his feet. He caught Bartelmo's arm and spun him round, pushing him hard. "Get away from here, you damned, no good goldbrick. I don't want to see Waco kill you."

Bartelmo staggered back. He stopped and glared at the others, knowing better than to try and fight Machie. His eyes glowed with hatred and his body was shaking with anger as he snarled:

"Fine bunch, you lot. Look at you, suckin' up to that black b——— like he was your long lost brother." He spat at Sam Bone, the saliva hitting the dark face.

Slowly, Sam came to his feet, rubbing the saliva with the back of his hand. His voice was cold, deadly and bitter. "Boy, you gone too far. I've took all I aims to from you. If you wants to do something make a start."

Bartelmo lunged forward, his fists driving at the older man's face. Just what happened next none of the recruits could say, although Waco, Doc and Machie knew what was happening. They all saw Sam Bone avoid the fists, then there was a tangle of arms; two bodies came together. Then Bartelmo was down on his stomach with Sam Bone standing astride his back, pulling his head back with two strong hands locked under his chin. That was an old Apache wrestling trick and a far more dangerous hold than many.

"Best give up, soldier," Waco warned. "Happen Sam drops down with his knee he's going to bust your back. I wouldn't want to have to tote even you back out of here like that."

Contemptuously Sam Bone let loose of the soldier and stepped back. Bartelmo rolled on to his back, then sat up, his hand went to his belt, starting to unclip the flap of the holster.

Machie stepped forward, dragged Bartelmo to his feet and hurled him towards the fire where he'd been sitting with his cronies. "You get back there and stay there. When we get back to the fort me'n ole Sergy O'Brien'll teach you some better manners."

Bartelmo returned to his own fire and sat down. The rest of his bunch, except for Davies, got to their feet and started to drift towards the other fire where the laughter was resumed amongst the men round it. Bartelmo made no attempt to say anything to them: he knew that they would not accept him as their leader any more. They thought he was tough and on two occasions he had been shown up by those two men. For a time he and Davies sat in moody silence.

"I'm sick of this whole lousy outfit," Bartelmo snarled. "Look at them, all of them, sucking round that nigger. They make me retch. I'm going over the hill tonight. We ain't likely to be going any further west; starting to swing north and then east again tomorrow. So I'm going to take my chance and go down over the border and work my way along to California. You coming with me?"

Davies thought this over. He admired Bartelmo, but he also knew that they were more at home in the city. Out here they were lost and would have a hard and hungry time of it. He also remembered what Waco and Doc had told them of Chacon's way with prisoners.

"Not me, Vin," he answered. "We don't know how to travel in this country and the Mexicans won't act friendly. You know what that Ranger told us the first night out?"

"He was lying, that's what he was doing," Bartelmo answered, seeing Davies weakening and not wanting to go alone. "You bet that shavetail told him to tell us all them lies to stop us deserting."

"I don't think he was."

Bartelmo saw that there would be no chance of getting Davies to go along with him so he snarled, "All right then. I'll go it alone. You give me all your ammunition, you won't need it and I might."

Without argument Davies emptied his pistol pouch and the bullets for his Springfield carbine, retaining only the bullet in the carbine's breech and the loads in the revolver. He did not expect to need the ammunition on this patrol as they had seen nothing to shoot at all the time they'd been out.

"When you going?" he asked.

"I'm standing guard from midnight, I'm going then," Bartelmo answered. He was wondering if there was a

chance of his killing either Sam Bone or the Ranger before
he went. This idea he gave up as impracticable: the shot
would wake up the camp and he would never get away.

The patrol went to sleep, rolled in their blankets and at
midnight Bartelmo was shaken awake and told to take his
turn of guard duty. He allowed a few minutes to go by
before he made for the horse lines and collected his horse.
He disturbed the other animals but, working fast, he saddled his horse, mounted and rode out of the camp.

Waco and Doc were sleeping side by side. They both
woke at the same moment, rolling from their blankets and
sat listening. Each of them held a gun and they came to
their feet; across the fire from them Machie was also sitting
up and looking round and Sam Bone was out of his blankets, fading into the blackness like a shadow.

Shaking Beaulieu awake, Waco hissed, "There's somebody just pulled out of camp."

The young officer showed his control over his nerves;
he did not make a sound for a moment, then replied, "Who
is it?"

Machie came to them and supplied the answer. "Bartelmo's gone over the hill."

Sam Bone arrived back to confirm the statement; he had
seen Bartelmo riding out but was too late to do anything
about it. However, he'd left his hat to serve as a marker for
the detail who would go after the deserter, saving them the
time of looking for tracks.

For a moment Beaulieu was silent, then he said, "We'll
have to send a detail out after him."

"Too dark to do a thing now," Waco answered. "Comes
dawn Doc and me'll go after him."

"Alone?"

"No, the two of us," then the levity left Waco's voice.
"You hold your men on the route we planned out this eve-

ning at daylight. Me'n Doc'll get on his trail and bring him back. If he comes up with either Chacon or any other Mexican bunch we'll have them down on us."

"You don't think they would attack an Army patrol this size?"

"Why not, they're bigger'n us and they'll know it if they meet Bartelmo."

"We don't know that Bartelmo would tell them anything." Beaulieu wanted to look at the best side of a fellow soldier against the civilians if he could.

"A man'll talk good and plenty with his feet shoved into a fire and a Yaqui skinning knife working under his hide," Doc answered. "Which same'll be mild to what they'll do if they don't get talk out of him and fast."

"Then when they know how many men are in the patrol they come alooking for it," Waco went on. "And they won't come whooping and yelling like a drunk Comanche headed for a pow-pow. When they come it'll be from ambush, trying to get as many of you as they can in the first volley."

"Ole Peludo can shoot: he's got him a Sharps Reliable that holds true at a mile and a half and for close work he's got one of these Winchester Centennial rifles. Took it from a storekeeper at Morenci. He'll show you that Mexicans can fight when he's ready and got his place picked out," Doc carried on.

"When he's got it picked you'll get a chance to use that shortgrowed wall gun there." Waco pointed to the weapon which was Beaulieu's pride and joy.

It was a sixteen inch barrelled Colt Peacemaker, the butt cut for an attachable, skeleton stock, making it either a revolver or a carbine. It was a present to the young officer from his mother and he was sure it would do great things although the two Texans scoffed at the idea. They pointed out that Ned Buntline presented five of those long-barrelled pistol-carbines to the Dodge City police force and none of that "noble" bunch of lawmen ever amounted to anything with the guns.

"If we see Chacon I'll shoot him a couple of times with my gun before he gets into range of your stingy guns," Beaulieu replied, although he knew that behind the banter the two young Texans were worried by the desertion. "Do you think we'll get him back?"

"Mister," Waco's voice lost all its levity and became grim. "We'd better get him back one way or another, and do it afore he falls in with the Mexicans."

Waco and Doc were in their saddles at the first light of dawn, riding along the line of tracks made by the departing soldier. Riding side by side they followed their usual routine when doing something like this. Waco followed the sign, reading it as easily as a professor would read a child's first primer. By his side, rifle across his knees ready for instant use, Doc kept his attention on the range ahead of them.

There was nothing hard, to a man of Waco's ability, in following the tracks left by Bartelmo. The soldier had left camp and headed south-west in a straight line, making no attempt to hide his sign. Even if he'd made the attempt, it would have taken a better man than the green soldier to mislead Waco.

For two hours they rode at an easy walk; Doc alert for possible ambush and Waco reading the sign. Then Doc brought his horse to a halt and pointed ahead. Hovering and circling in the sky were black shapes, and now and again one would swoop downwards then rocket up again.

"Buzzards. Could be him."

"Could be," Waco agreed. "I surely hope it isn't. If it is, then he and us have found bad trouble."

The deserter had found trouble, bad trouble, just as

Waco predicted. They found him lying spread-eagled on the ground, still tied to the pegs which were driven into the earth. Bartelmo was stripped to the waist, his feet still resting on the embers of a fire and with strips of skin removed from his torso. The Mexican bandits had tortured him, then shot him in the stomach as they left. Yet he was still alive, the rise and fall of his chest told them that. How he'd lived this long they did not know; he was barely conscious now, raving in delirium.

Waco made a wry face and rode his horse by the writhing body, swinging down from his saddle to go over the ground and learn what he could from the sign. What he saw gave him cause to worry. A large band of Mexicans had been here, camped, and from the sign, Bartelmo rode in like he was coming home for dinner. They'd pulled him from his horse and staked him out there. The rest he could imagine and shut the thought out of his head.

Doc bent over the writhing, gibbering man; then made out the words Bartelmo repeated over and over. The young Ranger straightened up, looking at his horse. In his warbag he carried a small case with a few surgical instruments; he was equipped to handle broken bones or bullet wounds. But there was nothing he could do for this man for he had neither the equipment nor the drugs to ease the pain. Bartelmo might lie in agony for a few moments or for hours, there was no way to relieve his sufferings. No way but one.

Doc stood still for a moment, then set his face hard and took out his revolver.

Waco heard the shot but did not turn round; there were some things a man did not want to look upon. He swung into the saddle and waited until Doc came alongside, afork his big black. The pallid face showed no expression at all, but Waco knew his friend was tense behind that expressionless mask.

"Bartelmo took it like a man. They near-to burned his feet off and skinned him. That means he held on as long as he could. He must have broke in the end and they put a bullet into him."

Waco gripped his partner's arm, squeezing it hard. "You couldn't have done a thing for him, the way he was. He was in agony and wouldn't ever have made it back to Orejano; couldn't have got him any place where a doctor could take care of him. The sooner I'm back with the blue bellies the happier I'll be."

"And me. Bartelmo kept muttering the regiment was out. That must have been what he was on about and told them. He might have been all kinds of a fool but he died like a man."

Waco considered this for a spell. Just long enough to put the Kelly petmakers to the flanks of his big paint and head it for the troop of cavalry.

Sam Bone rode alongside Beaulieu at the head of the patrol, keeping the men moving at a steady pace. They were riding along the bottom of a high cliff, following the now dry bed of what had been a large river. The other bank was a far more gentle slope, covered with rocks, cholla, prickly pear and stinkwood. The cliff wall was in places broken open by what must have been off-shoots of river, one of them, the largest they'd seen so far, was just ahead.

Sam Bone looked around, rolling his eyes and keeping his attention on the more gentle slope. It was the sort of place an Apache would pick to lay an ambush.

"I've got me a real bad hunch, suh," he said, licking his lips. "Real bad. Like the time we was hunting ole Geronimo. I got to feeling them Apaches was about."

"Well?"

"They was."

Sam gave his complete attention to that gentle slope again, scouring every inch of it, trying to locate something which would give him warning of danger ahead.

"You feel the same way now?" Beaulieu asked, also looking.

"I surely does, suh. Reckon you'd best slap the butt on that there long gun of your'n. Happen I'm right, there won't be time later on."

Beaulieu drew the long-barrelled revolver from the special holster on his saddle and from the back of the holster took the skeleton stock. He screwed the stock on to the butt and sat nursing the gun across his saddle. Looking back he saw Corporal Machie at the rear of the column ease back the hammer of his Springfield. Machie too sensed that all was not well and was alert and watchful.

"Any sign of the Rangers?" Beaulieu asked.

Sam twisted round in his old saddle and nodded. "They're coming now, suh. Looks like they found that young feller."

"He's not with them," Beaulieu answered, also turning.

"No suh, he ain't. That's why I reckon they found him. Too late."

Beaulieu raised his hand, halting the patrol just opposite the gap in the cliff. He waited for the Rangers to catch up and wondered what they'd found that was bringing them back in such a hurry.

Riding his big paint stallion at full gallop, Waco scanned the range ahead of him. On the slope above the patrol he saw a flash of colour where such a colour should not be. He fastened the reins to the saddlehorn, steering the paint with his knees and pulling the heavy Winchester rifle from his saddleboot. He brought the rifle up and fired, the bullet screaming off in a vicious ricochet just in front of the spot where the colour had showed for a moment.

From ahead of the patrol, appearing as if they'd come right out of the ground, came many Mexicans, all with rifles lining down on the soldiers. Lead screamed down at the soldiers and for a moment there was panic amongst the recruits; Davies screamed, clutched at his leg and slid from his saddle.

Beaulieu panicked for an instant himself, then regained a grip on his nerves and took command. Even as Machie opened his mouth to bellow orders the young officer shouted, "Up that gap there. Dismount and fight on foot."

The recruits whirled their horses and headed for the hole in the cliff, each man dropping from his saddle as the horses went through the gap and taking up whatever cover he could find. Two of them did not make it, despite the fact that Beaulieu, Machie and Sam Bone were giving them covering fire. The bullets cut round the men and as Beaulieu opened his mouth to tell the other two they could move in Machie was hit in the head and slid from his horse.

"Get back in there with your men, Lootenant," Sam yelled.

Beaulieu whirled his horse, a bullet tearing the campaign hat from his head as he went back. Sam Bone was about to follow when Davies, realising that he was being left out there, gave a wild screech and sat up.

Sam Bone spun the mule round and headed towards the soldiers, yelling for the patrol to give him covering fire. It was then that he saw the two Rangers barrelling down towards him and heard Waco's wild cry of:

"Comanche style, Sam."

Riding by Davies, Sam Bone turned his mule and started it forward. The mule was an old, baulky and ornery beast but he knew that when guns roared and lead sang in the air he must obey every command without objection. He lunged forward at a good speed and behind came the rapid thunder of hooves. Sam Bone bent in the saddle, hand reaching down to take hold of Davies' right arm; then from the corner of his eye the Negro saw the huge paint alongside and Waco leaning over to grab the other blue-clad arm. Davies felt himself lifted up and with feet dragging was pulled along between the racing animals.

The Mexicans tried to concentrate their fire on this tempting target, but from under the cliff Beaulieu, exposing himself recklessly, directed a savage covering fire, possessed in his attempt to prevent any Mexican getting a clear shot at Waco.

Through a hail of screaming lead Waco and Sam Bone dragged Davies into the comparative safety of the hole in the cliff. Waco let the soldier fall to the ground again and looked round him. Just how this place was formed he did not know, but it was not what he would have chosen. The hole led into a valley which went back for some hundred yards, then ended in a steep wall. All the valley amounted to was a pocket in the cliff face. There was some grass growing in the pocket, but no water that Waco could see.

Doc joined his friend, examining a hole in his coat and condemning all greasers to eternal damnation. The pallid young man bent over Davies and looked at the bullet wound. From the position of the hole and the fact that Davies could move his leg Doc knew the bullet had missed bone and gone right through. He straightened up and went to his horse, opening his warbag and taking out the box with the surgical instruments.

Davies was sitting up, holding his leg. He looked at Doc, then to where Sam Bone was kneeling alongside Waco, working an old Henry rifle.

"The nigger came back and saved me," he said.

"Sure," Doc agreed. "Now if I'd been Sam I'd have let you lie there in case I was taking some white man's work toting you back in. Here, let me look at that leg."

With Davies attended to, Doc went back, keeping in what cover he could find until he settled down behind the large rock where Beaulieu, Waco and Sam Bone were kneeling. The young officer held his long-barrelled Colt and was putting bullets in the loading gate as he turned the chamber. Doc regarded the weapon with disgust and scoffed:

"Likely he aims to lean over and poke ole Chacon right in the eye."

"Can't," Waco replied. "Old Peludo ain't with that bunch."

"You been over and asked them?"

"Don't need to, Doc. If Chacon was there this ambush'd been better set out than it was. He wouldn't have left a place like this open for us. When you brought your boys in here, Beau, you'd have found rifles waiting for you. That bunch out there aren't up to Chacon's style of work."

Beaulieu was willing to accept Waco's judgment of the situation and he had an idea the young Texan would prove right. He looked up at the sheer wall of the cliff and asked: "Is there any way they can get above us?"

"Not for a couple of miles, Lootenant, not on a hoss," Sam Bone answered. "I know this wall here. It goes on for mebbe five miles and for two it's like this, too steep for a hoss."

"Too steep for that ole mule of your'n Sam?" Waco asked with a grin. "You been telling us all along it's part goat and can climb like a cat."

"Ole General Ambilech could get up it and down in a couple of places," Sam replied. "Why'd you ask?"

"Just curious," Waco answered.

"Could the Mexicans get above us?" Beaulieu inquired.

"Sure, but they won't," Waco replied with confidence. "Not if it means doing it on foot. They don't need to. All the water we've got is in the canteens; they can wait until thirst drives us out. Never saw a Mexican who'd take the hard way to do anything, not when there was an easy way of doing it."

"How about at night?"

"Depends on how well they know the country. Put yourself in their position. They've got us pinned down and they're moving along to get in better places." Waco pointed to the darting shapes as Mexicans moved from cover to cover until they got in positions opposite the soldiers. "Would you pull even half of your men out and send them wandering round in the dark, climbing that wall there when you can get all you want without any of that trouble?"

Beaulieu smiled at the thought of this civilian giving him a lecture on military tactics. He gave an order to his men not to shoot unless they were sure of a hit, for some of the recruits were firing every time a Mexican showed himself. The firing died away on this side of the valley, but the Mexicans kept firing at the rocks in an attempt to make the soldiers waste ammunition.

"I wouldn't," the officer finally agreed.

"Nor would they. Besides, like I said, a Mexican will never do anything the hard way when he can do it easy. How about—"

"Gringos, hey gringos!" a voice shouted from the other side. "Come on out, leave us your money and your guns and you can go free. We don't want to harm you."

"You want our guns come on over and get them," Waco yelled back. "But you watch the other soldiers don't get you."

This caused something of a sensation amongst the Mexicans, several of them gathered together in a bunch well up on top of the other slope. All were talking and there were shouted inquiries in Spanish which Doc and Waco translated for the benefit of Beaulieu. It was Doc who explained about Bartelmo's story of the regiment being out. The Mexicans appeared to be taking it seriously, but they did not show any signs of calling off the attack until some sign of reinforcements showed.

Beaulieu called one of his men, the oldest soldier amongst the recruits, and told him off to collect all the canteens, then place a guard on them. He then made the rounds of his men, darting from cover to cover and risking death at each move. With each man he stayed for a time, talking to them and raising their spirits. With this done he returned to Waco, Doc and Sam, who'd been watching him with some admiration.

"Reckon you'd best have that bugler of your'n sound a few calls through the day, like he was calling to the other soldiers," Waco suggested.

"And you've been saying all along that he was a waste of time," Beaulieu replied. "Do you reckon we could make a run for it?"

"Not without losing at least half of the patrol," Waco replied. "We'd best stay where we are for now."

"After that?"

"Waal, I'll tell you. For a choice I'd rather go out fighting than be captured by that bunch over there."

For the rest of the day the Mexicans held down a steady and desultory fire on the soldiers, doing no damage and causing no casualties. The aim of the bandits was to hold down the gringos until proof that the rest of the regiment were or were not out. If the regiment was out, the Mexicans would head for the border fast. If not, well odds of two to one were just what the bandits liked.

Night came down and across the valley fires sprang up, lighting the area in front of the pocket even though there was no moon. Waco guessed this would happen and warned Beaulieu that there would be no wild rush out into the night as they had hoped might be presented to them. The soldiers pulled back into the pocket as being easier to guard; sentries were put out and the rest of the men stood down, but without fires.

Just before they turned in for the night, Waco and Sam Bone held a conference; what they talked about none of the others knew. The recruits and Beaulieu got little sleep that night, but when they were not taking their turn at rounds, Waco and Doc rolled in their blankets and slept soundly.

"Sam Bone's gone!"

Waco rolled out of his blankets in the cold light of dawn and looked up at Beaulieu. The young officer pointed to where Sam had tethered his mule the night before.

"Lit out, huh?"

"Yes, I thought he might have stuck by us. He even took the bugle along."

Waco did not reply. He went to the edge of the pocket and looked across to where the Mexicans were taking up their places.

"Did you know he'd gone?"

"Why sure, I heard him."

"Why didn't you try and stop him?"

"No need. Like I told you last night me, Doc or Sam could likely get up that face and head back to Orejano, it wouldn't do the rest of us any good at all. Long afore we could make it there and get reinforcements fetched from the Fort the greasers would have us. 'Sides, me'n Doc couldn't get a hoss up there and I surely can't see us walking far in these boots."

Beaulieu watched Waco, wondering why the young Texan was watching the other side of the valley so carefully. He could not understand the young Texan's attitude at Sam Bone's desertion. Beaulieu opened his mouth to ask a question then saw a Mexican rise and point off along the valley.

"Get your men mounted!" There was urgency in Waco's voice. "Pronto!"

"What do you mean?" Beaulieu asked.

"Move, mister, we're going into the attack. We're going out of here whooping and hollering fit to bust, and shooting."

"You seen something we missed, boy?" Doc asked.

"Mebbe. Happen I call this wrong you can cuss me out. If Saint Peter allows cussing up here."

Beaulieu stared as Waco ran back and tightened the girths of his paint's saddle, then swung up. There was an urgency about the Texan that brooked no delay and put direction into the limbs of the soldiers. They grabbed their horses, one of them heaving Davies into his saddle before mounting himself. All eyes were on the tall young Texan who sat at the head of the pocket, a gun in either hand.

The Mexicans were getting excited, men running backwards and forwards and pointing off, while shouting to each other.

"Yeeah!"

The rebel yell shattered the air, throwing back echoes against the walls of the pocket. With that yell Waco put the petmakers to his paint, causing it to leap forward like the devil after a yearling. Beaulieu roared out, "Charge!"

For once in his life, in the brief, whirling second after he left the mouth of the pocket, Waco thought he'd made a bad mistake. Looking along in the direction the Mexicans were staring he saw dust rising; far too much dust for one lone man mounted on a mule. If he'd called this play wrong he'd soon know, for Mexican lead would cut him down.

Then from the fast-rolling cloud of dust came the most beautiful sound Waco had ever heard. A bugle screaming the wild, mad notes of the charge.

That was all the Mexicans wanted to hear. They saw the soldiers coming at them, led by the wild Tejano on a wild-eyed horse and with a brace of roaring guns in his hands. Then they heard the bugle and knew that the captured soldier spoke truly, the regiment was out. A fair portion of it was coming this way. Enough to narrow the odds against the men they'd ambushed.

The slope was crowded with running Mexicans, bounding up to the top and heading for their horses as fast as they could go. There was no sight in the world so guaranteed to rouse a soldier as the backs of a fleeing enemy and those recruits reacted like veterans. They cut down on the running Mexicans, sending them rolling in the dirt.

At the top of the slope Waco roared, "Beau, call them off!"

Beaulieu stared wildly at Waco, then back at the rapid riding Mexicans, scattering and heading for the border as fast as they could go. Then the mad fighting light died from his eyes, and like a bugle call his voice rang out.

"Re-form on me. Re-form the troop."

It took some time to cool the fight-mad soldiers down, but at last they were under control again. Flushed and grinning at each other they assembled, all eager to tell each other of the part they had taken in the fight.

"What happened?" Beaulieu turned to Waco. "Where did the other troop come from?"

"Over there. Colonel Bone and his one man, one mule army."

Sam Bone rode up, one hand holding the bugle, the other patting his mule's neck. From his saddlehorn was a rope and at the end of it, still stirring up dust, was a big clump of mesquite. His face was split by a grin that almost stretched from ear to ear and he raised his hand in a salute.

Waco held out a hand, gripping Sam's and asked,

"Why'd you do that. You like to scared me out of a year's growth when I saw that dust."

"You mean you knew all along that Sam was out there?" Beaulieu asked, eyeing the two grinning men. "Why didn't you say?"

"I didn't know if he'd make it at all. We fixed it together. Sam took ole General Ambilech up the face there where a hoss couldn't have gone. He was supposed to stay back out of sight and blow calls. Looks like he thought his own idea out and tried it."

"What now, Lootenant?" Sam Bone asked.

"Form a burial detail for our men and then carry on looking for Chacon."

"Won't do any good at all," Waco answered. "Chacon isn't out."

"How can you be so sure?"

"Ole Peludo's like a silvertip grizzly. He hunts with his bunch and he won't let no other bunch hunt his balliwick. That crowd there weren't fit to wipe Chacon's boots; they'd never work any place where he was likely to be."

Beaulieu looked at the still shapes on the hill, then at Waco and Doc. "I reckon you're right, like always," he said.

The patrol returned to Orejano by the shortest route. There was confirmation and proof of Waco's judgment waiting for them in the shape of a message from Captain Mosehan. Waco read it then handed it to Beaulieu.

"Chacon seen on New Mexico line; return to Tucson as fast as possible or even faster."

The young officer turned to Sam Bone. They were at the door of his small shop and the troop were lined up ready to move out again.

"Forgot to ask you, Sam. Where did you learn to blow the bugle?"

"Was the bestest bugler my regiment ever had, suh," Sam answered.

One of the soldiers turned to Davies and snorted. "You said Sam didn't fight in the war, didn't you?"

Beaulieu gave the order and the troop rode by the three men, the answer Davies gave being lost to them.

"I'm sure pleased they didn't ask me what regiment," Sam Bone remarked. He stepped into the building and came out carrying an Army uniform.

It was Confederate grey, not Union blue.

The Bail Jumpers

The small wooden building on the outskirts of Tucson was neither large nor impressive; just a single storey, four-room building behind a once white fence. At the back was a small storehouse and a corral with a few very good horses in it. A painted sign read, to the old woman who'd walked by twice and now halted there, "Arizona Rangers, Captain Bertram H. Mosehan."

Hesitantly she pushed open the gate and walked up the path, pausing to look back nervously before she halted at the door. She braced herself and pushed open the door, walking into a small office. At a desk, trying to decipher a report written by a man who only very rarely held a pen, was a slim, handsome young man in his shirt sleeves.

He looked up and rose as the woman came towards him.

"Good afternoon, ma'am." His accents were not those of the range. "Can I help you?"

"I want to see Bertram Mosehan. Tell him Minnie Thornton is here; he'll see me quick enough."

Jed Peters was a young man with a keen memory and the name meant something to him. He turned and went to the door immediately behind his chair, knocked on it and entered.

"I think we've got a break at last, Captain," he said, looking at Waco and Doc Leroy who were lounging at the side of the room. "Mrs. Thornton is outside."

"Fetch her in, Jed," Mosehan replied, then looked at the two Texans who were putting on their hats. "Stay and listen. It might be the chance we've been waiting for."

Waco and Doc settled back again. They'd been brought in from their more usual area of operations up at Backsight in Coconino County to help on this serious and unfruitful chore in the south. Someone here was running the small freighting outfits out of business, making them pay protection money and gradually forcing them out. The Governor came to hear of this and assigned his Captain of Rangers to break the hold of the gang. So far without success, Mosehan and his two Tucson men, Glendon and Speed, tried to get a lead. None of the small freight outfits would talk or cooperate, being afraid of repercussions, so Mosehan brought in the two men who were rapidly becoming his tophands to help out.

He came up and crossed to greet the sturdy old woman in the black mourning clothes. "I am real sorry to hear about ole Dad, Aunt Minnie," he said, escorting her to a chair. "That's why you've come to see me, isn't it?"

"It is. The local law can't help us and I wouldn't want Pinkertons on it. I heard you was head of the Arizona Rangers and came down here. You wanted someone to tell you who's been driving all the small freighters out of business?"

"We want somebody who'll go into a witness box and say it," Mosehan replied.

"And that'll be me." Minnie Thornton's voice was grim. "You know that two of their best men beat up Dad and he died through it. I was in bed ill at the time but I got out and saw them finishing off. I couldn't even get downstairs for my shot gun to help them out. But I saw them and I'd recognise them again."

"Do you know their names, ma'am?" Waco asked gently, seeing how the woman was fighting down her grief.

"No, but I'd know them again. They were tall, heavy-built men and they was wearing dude clothes. I'd swear they wasn't range men."

"Were they, either of them, the man who came to see you first?" Mosehan asked. "We know how the game's being run but not by whom."

"No, it wasn't him. He was a dude like them, but smaller. Kinda dark skinned like he'd got Mex blood in him. They didn't look like him at all. He came and saw me and Dad first, told us he wanted fifty dollars a week protection. We paid it."

"Freighters don't usually scare that easy, ma'am," Doc put in.

"He didn't threaten Dad; it was me and our gal over in Bisbee they said they'd hurt. That was why Dad paid up. But that wasn't the end of it. They came round and told us to fire all our old hands and take on their men. Dad wouldn't do it. He got word to our gal and she went East for a vacation. I was in bed ill and they beat him up. Like I say, I only saw the end of it. They killed him."

"And that's being done all over the south of the Territory," Mosehan explained. "Which is why I brought you two in. You're not so well-known down here as Pete and Billy. The Governor's heard about this game and wants to holler keno on it. It's been going on a piece; the original owners tried to fight and they ended up in what looked like accidents. The freighters wouldn't talk; every time it was the same, the protection bunch went for their kin, threatened to hurt their wives or daughters. A man'll take chances with himself, but not with his family. So they were run out of business."

"Who buys the businesses up?"

"Nobody so far. There is a big freight outfit called Carelli's Freight Services putting a branch into each town. They operate cheaper than the small outfit that went out of business; start doing it as soon as the small bunch go out. They might be tied in with this gang or they might not. There's no proof either way."

"They've just started operating in Tucson."

The three Rangers looked at the old woman; it was Waco who asked, "How'd you know that, ma'am?"

"I saw the man who came to see us first today. I was just going along to see young Hal Maxim and I saw him leaving their place. I kept out of sight until he'd gone, then went round to see Hal and his wife. They were scared and they wouldn't talk about it at first. I tried to get them to come round and see you Rangers but they daren't do it. Molly wanted Hal to, but he's scared of what they'll do to her. He said the man'd come round and told him to fire off all his men. The men are scared; things have happened to men who tried to stay on. They all wanted out."

There was silence again. Mosehan lifted his feet on to his desk and looked at the roof, a sure sign he was thinking. Waco sat handrolling a smoke, whistling a cattlesong. Doc went to the window and looked out along the street, seeing a few women walking towards the centre of town but nothing suspicious. The woman watched them without speaking. She knew that the Rangers would try to help her and was satisfied that they were going to take a hand.

Mosehan's feet came down from the desk and he stood up. Waco knew his chief very well and looked up with a grin.

"You got something, Cap'n Bert?"

"I need a man who can handle his fists and isn't scared to leave his guns off for a spell. It could be dangerous even though I'll have him covered all the time."

Doc turned from the window, eyes going to his handsome, wide-shouldered young friend and a smile on his face.

"When do you start, boy?" he asked.

The small, thin man in the town clothes pointed to the wagon standing in front of Maxim's Freight Yard. A tall, blond young man was checking the wheels, a man with the sleeves of his blue shirt rolled up, old blue jeans, high-heeled boots and no gun.

"All right, Kagg, Bunt. That's the one. Work him over, the rest have all quit. Make sure you scare any more that might come."

"All right," Kagg, the bigger and heavier of the pair replied. "What you going to do while we're doing it?"

"You know what I'm going to do," the small man answered. "I mustn't be seen or connected with you at all."

"Can't say I like it, Maiden," Bunt, the second man, growled. "If we're caught who'll get us out of it?"

"You don't have to get caught. You know as well as I do that Mr. Carelli will not get involved in this. He told you that you were on your own the whole time. He can't afford to risk becoming involved with the other side."

"Carelli told us that," Kagg replied. "We don't like it all that much."

"The pay's good, don't forget."

"That's why we took on." Kagg watched the thin man. "We met Tull and Haufman down in Mexico and they told us about Carelli. They killed a man didn't they?"

Maiden nodded. He looked around, not wishing to be

seen with these two men; Carelli was strict on matters like
that. The agent in the town was to act as contact man but
never participate in any of the strong arm stuff. That was
what this kind of man was hired to do. The agent must
never allow himself to be seen with them and only came
out when there was an emergency like this. The two new
men did not know Tucson, and Maiden came to show them
the Maxim Freight Yard, keeping to the backstreets. He
wanted to get away before he was seen by someone.

"They killed a man all right. Didn't mean to but he was
old and couldn't stand the beating. So the boss told them to
get out of the country. Sent them down to Tejanus with
enough money to hold them until he needs them here
again. When you've done this you head down there and
wait with them. That way the law can't touch you. They
can't follow you into Mexico."

Maiden turned and hurried off. The other two let him
get out of sight before they moved forward, making for the
wagon and the young man who was working at it.

"Hey you!"

Waco straightened up and turned round. The two men
coming towards him wore range clothes and certainly were
not eastern dudes. They were both almost as tall and heavier than him, yet he guessed guns would be their weapons
and not fists.

"Me?" Waco's voice was mild, his face showing no expression at all.

"You," Kagg answered, moving nearer. "This ain't a
healthy company to work for."

"Why not?"

"Accidents happen to folk who work for it, don't they,
Bunt?"

"All the time, Kagg. All the time. You'd better quit,
sonny, afore one happens to you."

"What sort of accident, gents?"

"This sort!"

Kagg's fist shot out, a savage punch powered by all his weight. If it had landed Waco would have been in bad shape, but, as he guessed, Kagg was more used to handling a gun than his fists. The punch was slow and telegraphed to Waco's lightning-fast fighting impulses. His head moved aside, allowing the fist to whistle by his ear. The force of the swing brought Kagg forward, right on to Waco's left fist which shot out and drove into flesh like a mule kick. Kagg grunted and doubled up; Waco's knee came up, driven with all his strength to smash right into the man's face; he felt the nose squash under the impact. Then Kagg stood erect, clutching at his injured nasal organ, and staggered back.

Before Bunt could recover from his surprise, Waco came in fast, his right shooting out and exploding on Bunt's jaw. Bunt's head rocked back, then a left and a right rocked it back and forwards so fast that the man did not know if he was coming or going. He staggered back and Waco came in with a right to the bristly jaw which laid Bunt down on the ground.

Kagg, snarling curses and holding his nose with his left hand, started to pull his gun with his right. He saw a slim, lithe shape leap from the wagon and land by the side of the tall, blond youngster. A white hand made a flickering movement and a gun was lined on Kagg. At the same moment the door of the office was thrown open and three men came out, all holding guns.

"Rangers here, throw them high!"

It was a challenge that was meant to be obeyed. The two men were not from Arizona Territory but they knew that the Rangers never gave a challenge unless they expected to have it obeyed. Both Kagg and Bunt made their living by selling their guns to the highest bidder and they knew skilled gunhands when they saw them.

Kagg's hand came from his gunbelt and lifted to join the other which was also raised. On the floor Bunt shook off his daze and saw the futility of trying to match guns with these four men all alert and ready. He pushed himself to his feet and raised his hands, standing by his partner and scowling.

Waco moved behind the two men, coming in and taking their guns from them. He did it fast and with such skill that neither was given any chance of making a move. Then he caught the two sets of handcuffs Mosehan threw to him. Reaching up he pulled Kagg's arms down behind the big man's back and snapped the handcuffs on. Pushing Kagg towards the waiting Rangers, Waco handcuffed Bunt in the same manner, then said, "We'll get them down to the office by the back way."

Mosehan nodded in agreement. "I'll collect the witness after I've thanked Hal and his wife." He went into the office where a man and a woman sat behind the desk. "We got them both. From now until we've broke this thing Pete and Billy will stay with you all the time. I've got two more men coming in today to help me out and I can spare both Pete and Billy."

Hal Maxim looked up, some of the anxiety leaving his face. "I shouldn't be taking your men. I can—"

"You and Mrs. Thornton's our witnesses. We get three of you to testify and a lot of others will stand up and say their piece too. I'm leaving two men to watch you. Just do what they say and everything will be all right."

The young woman got up and came round the desk. "Hal wanted to come to you right away. But they said they'd hurt me if he did and Hal wouldn't risk it."

"I know that, it's the way this kind work. They go for

the women because they know they can't frighten the men any other way. Don't worry, we'll get them."

Mosehan returned to his headquarters, going into his office after seeing Mrs. Thornton, who was using the living room at the back. He gave her certain instructions and although she did not quite understand why she was to do the thing asked, she was willing to carry on and do it.

In the office Kagg and Bunt stood against the wall, sullen, brooding looks on their faces. Waco and Doc were seated at the desk and Jed Peters, notebook in hand, stood at the side of the door.

"What do we charge these two with, Captain?" he asked.

"Assault, attempted murder and murder."

It took a couple of seconds for the words to sink into the not overbright minds of Kagg and Bunt. Then they realised what Mosehan had said.

"Murder?" Bunt yelped like a beestung dog.

"What murder?" Kagg's voice was pitched high.

"Dad Thornton over Ysaleta way."

Kagg and Bunt looked at each other, relief showing plainly on their faces. That murder was one crime they definitely were not connected with.

"You reckon you can make it stick?" Kagg asked triumphantly.

"Got us a witness, friend," Waco replied. "She saw the two men and can identify them. If she recognises you, reckon we'll make her stick."

The two men sat at the desk, in the chairs where Waco put them, watching the door. Neither of them expected the woman to identify them; they were grinning at each other and waiting for the shock the Rangers were going to get. The other charge of attempted assault did not unduly worry them, for they felt that a good lawyer could get them out of it with no trouble.

The door opened and Mosehan came in with the old woman. Mrs. Thornton looked at Kagg and Bunt for a time, the grins dying from their faces and worry replacing them as the old woman looked them over.

"It's them all right, Captain," she finally said.

"She's lying!" Kagg screamed and came to his feet.

Waco put a hand over the man's face and shoved him back down into his seat, then turned to the old woman who stood by Mosehan's side. "You sure of that, ma'am?"

"Sure enough. I told you what the two looked like, except for the clothes these two are the same size."

Before either Kagg or Bunt could make a sound of protest, Mrs. Thornton was let out of the room and Mosehan looked the two men over. He did not speak for a moment, then said, "That closes it for us."

"I tell you we never done the killing," Kagg howled. "She's made a mistake. We weren't in Arizona when the killing was done."

"How do you know?" Doc's words cut across like a whip.

"We know the men who killed the old-timer. We met them down there and they told us when they done it." Kagg looked at the unsmiling faces, reading their disbelief. He stared wildly at Bunt, trying to remember exactly where they'd been when the killing took place, and failing.

"Who hired you?" Waco snapped.

Once more Kagg and Bunt looked at each other, remembering what Carelli had told them when he hired them. He'd warned them that any attempt at bringing him into it would end in failure. He'd promised that he would get them a good lawyer if they did get into trouble, but only if they kept him out of it.

"We was only having a joke with the Ranger," Bunt answered.

"All right, then we'll take you to Ysaleta for trial," Mosehan answered.

"Surely hope it gets to trial. Folks liked ole Dad down there. They likely will want the men who did it hanging from a tree without bothering with a trial."

"I tell you we didn't kill the old-timer," Kagg roared. "I want a lawyer."

"You can have one at Ysaleta, not before," Mosehan answered. "You've been identified as the killer and that's good enough for me. I'll have you sent there in the morning."

Waco moved nearer the table. "You know, Cap'n, there might be something in what they say. Why'd whoever hired them take them on. They looked like the two men who did the killing. Their boss knows that, sends them here to Tucson because he knows we'll take them to Ysaleta for trial and knows the mob will get them. Knows us and the local law won't face down and kill honest men to save the two who murdered Dad Thornton. So this pair get lynched and he can fetch his other boys back."

Kagg and Bunt's eyes met; they could see now it was pointed out to them that the young Ranger might be right. Both knew that Carelli took them on without knowing a thing about them and in something of a hurry. Now they could see there might be another motive than just needing two musclemen to carry on for Tull and Haufman who were lying low in Mexico.

"The lousy skunk," Bunt snarled. "The dirty, scent-smelling greaser."

"Yeah!" Kagg looked at the Rangers. "I'm not getting hung for him. The man you want is Carelli. You know, he runs that new freight outfit that's coming up so fast.

Maiden, his agent here, was the man we were told to report to. He took us and pointed you out to us. He must have known who you was and set us up."

"Could have at that," Waco agreed, then looked at Mosehan. "Do we take the said Mr. Maiden?"

"Go get him, Doc. Take Billy Speed and leave him to watch that no one sends a message off to Carelli. You two want to make a statement, talk ahead and Jed here can take it down."

By the time Maiden was collected and brought to Ranger headquarters, Kagg and Bunt had told all they knew, putting it down in the statement and signing it. They looked up with glowering eyes at the thin man as he was escorted into the room by Doc Leroy. Maiden's face was a dead giveaway as he stared at the two men, then he managed to get hold of himself and asked:

"What did you want to see me about, Captain Mosehan?"

"These men say you can clear them on a murder charge."

"I never saw them before in my life. I don't know them and I don't know a thing about Dad Thornton's killing."

"Who said anything about Dad Thornton?" Waco snapped.

"I—I—I—" Maiden stared at the men, realising he'd made a bad slip. "I never saw these two men before in my life."

"They said you could clear them of a murder charge, friend," Waco put in. "How about it, why'd they mention you?"

"I don't know why." Maiden stared round at the men again; he was getting panicky, for he'd never expected to be caught in this business. "I want to see my lawyer. This is an outrage."

"Why'd you want a lawyer?" Mosehan asked. "We haven't charged you with anything yet."

Waco turned to Kagg and Bunt. "Sorry, gents. Looks like we'll have to take you to Ysaleta after all, this gent hasn't cleared you."

Kagg lunged forward, his foot driving up at Maiden. At the same moment Bunt charged forward, his shoulder smashing into the thin man and knocking him backwards. Waco grabbed Kagg by the shirt collar and heaved him backwards, while Mosehan pushed Bunt to one side.

With a snarl that was half fear, half terror, Maiden sent his arm under his coat and brought out a short-barrelled Colt Storekeeper revolver. Doc Leroy's ivory-butted Colt came out and smashed down on to the man's gun arm hard. With a moan of agony Maiden let the gun fall and clutched at his injured arm, going to his knees.

"All right," Mosehan snapped. "We're holding you on a charge of attempted murder, Maiden. Put the prisoners in the cells out back."

"Only got one spare cell, Cap'n," Waco remarked cheerfully. "I'll take the handcuffs off these two and put them in; Doc bring the other one."

Maiden realised what was being said; he also realised how he would be situated, locked in a cell with those two men whose life he held in his hands. They would get the truth out of him one way or another. He suspected that the Rangers were going to let Kagg and Bunt do just that and knew that his only chance was to talk and talk fast.

"All right, all right," he gasped. "I'll talk, I'll make a statement and sign it. Just don't lock me with these two. They didn't kill Dad Thornton."

Half an hour later the telegraph wires began to sing and in a dozen towns the local law moved fast. The orders came, not from the Arizona Rangers, but from the Gover-

nor of the Territory himself. The agent of Carelli's Freight
Services in each town was arrested and held incommuni-
cado; the men who worked for the company kept away
from telegraph offices. Other law enforcement officers
went round the various ruined freight owners and with
guarantees of protection obtained full particulars of the
men who'd scared or put them out of business.

In Tucson, Mosehan, Federal Judge Carmody and the
Governor's legal staff were kept very busy sifting the information which came in to them. It was noon the following day before Mosehan called in Waco, Doc Leroy, Pete
Glendon and Billy Speed.

"Go to Calverton, that's the head office of the Carelli
Freight Services."

"Sure, Cap'n," Waco answered. "Then what?"

"Arrest Carelli, Dodd and Spencer, they run the company and they're the ones we want. The Governor'll in-
demnify you against any measures you take in the arrest.
He wants them and he wants them bad."

Luigi Carelli was at peace with the world as he ushered his
guests from the room and watched the cream of Calverton
society walking along the hotel passage. Then he shut the
door and went back to the table. Carelli was a short, fat
Italian, dressed to the height of good taste and latest fashion of the East. Dodd, his second in command, was a big,
burly man, always talking loud and making jokes. He was
the mixer, the man who raised goodwill amongst the men-
folk by heartiness and a hand which willingly shot out to
pick up the check when in company. Spencer, the third
partner, was smaller, a sober-looking man who attended
church regularly, three times every Sunday, and was
always on hand when the reverend held out his palm for
donations. It was Spencer who kept the ladies of the town

in hand, they pointed him out and held him up as a shining
example of the ideal man.

Each of the trio had his part to play. Carelli was the
shrewd business head of the organisation. Circumstances,
including the New York police, sent him west to what
proved to be a land of milk and honey. He'd brought his
two partners with him and they picked on the freight business as being the one which would afford them the best
chance. The first step was to establish themselves in Calverton, to make friends with the people who counted, the
banker, the county sheriff, the richer merchants. By careful
working the three were now regarded as being the most
desirable of citizens and a stranger who might have passed
a disparaging remark about them would be likely to wind
up in jail.

The door closed and from the bedroom where he'd been
waiting came a dark, swarthy man, dressed in clothes more
suited to New York's tough East Side then here in Arizona
Territory. Under his arm he carried a saddle pouch; this he
put on the table and opened it.

"How's it going, Toni?" Carelli asked.

"Not bad, boss. We got another tough one on our hands,
over Bisbee way. He ain't got no family and he's real
tough."

"Fix him."

"No killing, Fascati!" Dodd warned. "We don't want
any more killing if we can help it. Get those two new men
on it, work him over or burn his place."

Spencer, the legal mind of the trio, looked at the pouch
and said the same thing he'd said many times before.

"I don't like the idea of Fascati bringing that pouch
here. There's enough in it to get us all in jail for the rest of
our lives."

"Don't worry, Albert," Carelli answered. "Nobody

knows we're connected with Toni here. In this town they'd
never believe anything bad about us. Why if we were arrested I bet those bunch who just left would write to the
Governor and demand we were let loose."

"I know, but it seems foolish to take such a chance—"
Spencer protested feebly, watching Fascati spread out on
the table enough evidence to send them all to Yuma, a far
less pleasant place than any prison they'd been in back
East.

The door burst open and two men came in, guns in
hand.

"Rangers here, throw them high!"

Carelli, Dodd and Spencer were seated, Fascati standing
with his back to the door. Not one of them had the time or
the opportunity to do anything and only Fascati was armed.
He twisted round, hand going up under his arm in the misguided belief that his speed on the draw could beat the
guns in the hands of those two tall, young Texas men. Like
most of his kind, he regarded the Western lawmen as un-
trained, unintelligent country hicks, easily fooled and an
easy mark. His gun skill was famous in New York against
his opponents, the New York police, who in those days
relied far more on the nightstick than the gun and were far
from being efficient and well-trained performers. Fascati
was fast by New York standards; but Calverton, Arizona,
was not New York and went by a different standard.

Even with his guns in leather Waco could have beaten
Fascati to the shot, with them out he could find time to
pick his mark and sent a .45 bullet through the dude's
shoulder. The force of the bullet, powered by thirty grains
of prime Dupont powder, sent shock waves ripping through
him and dropped him to the ground, his gun sliding from
his hand.

"Freeze all of you!" Waco snapped. "We're Arizona Rangers."

"What do you want?" Carelli had a very low opinion of the abilities and morals of Western lawmen and these two looked even younger than most. "We've a warrant for your arrest on charges of extortion, accessory before and after murder," Doc replied. He could hear doors opening and people running towards the room.

Spencer stared at the buff-coloured paper Doc Leroy held out, knowing all too well what it was. He looked down at the papers on the desk and his face paled, knowing that they were caught well and truly.

Dodd suddenly roared. "Hold up in here!" and dived for the gun on the floor.

Waco's left-hand Colt crashed out, the bullet hitting the revolver and knocking it from under Dodd's hand. The man crashed to the floor and lay there, hand outstretched, waiting for a bullet to strike him.

The footsteps halted in the hall, none of the people who'd come out of the rooms making any attempt to come in. They were halted by two hard-faced, unsmiling men who informed them, from behind lined guns, that this was not a hold-up but that the Arizona Rangers were making an arrest.

For a moment Carelli was silent; the sudden arrival of the two Rangers and the casual, easy way they'd handled Fascati, whom Carelli regarded as being very good with a gun, unnerved him. He was, for once, taken by surprise and off balance. Dodd's failure to get assistance did not help Carelli to assess his position any better. He knew that these men were not local law and knew they wielded considerably more power than either the county sheriff or the town marshal.

"How much money do you boys make a month?" he asked.

"Enough," Waco replied. "Doc, get Pete in here and collect all those papers on the table."

Carelli and his two partners were forced back against the wall; Pete Glendon and Billy Speed came in, handcuffs were clipped on and the incriminating papers collected. They were doing this when someone knocked hard on the door and a voice roared:

"Open up. Sheriff here."

Waco opened the door and the sheriff came in, face flushed with the exertion for running back to the hotel after the meal Carelli had laid out before him and his fellow citizens. He came in, two deputies at his back, followed by the town marshal who was also red-faced and puffing hard.

"What's all this?" he asked.

Waco holstered his guns and held out the warrant without a word. The sheriff read the warrant through, then handed it to the town marshal.

"There's been a mistake somewhere," he snapped. "Release Mr. Carelli."

"Sure, as soon as he's safe in a cell," Waco replied.

"Not in my jail," the marshal snapped. "I ain't having you Rangers coming into my town and—"

"Take a look at this, friend," Waco answered, holding out a letter.

The marshal took the letter, glanced at the printed heading, then gulped and read the writing underneath.

"This is from the Governor," he finally said.

"Sure, asking for full co-operation from the County Sheriff and Town Marshal," Waco answered. "What was you saying?"

The town marshal scowled, being awkward with the Arizona Rangers was not a safe game to play at any time.

When they bore a letter from the Governor asking that every assistance and facility be given to the said Rangers it was like patting a teased-up and riled rattler.

"This's a misunderstanding, Mr. Carelli," the sheriff remarked. "I'm afraid that our hands are tied and that you must come down to the jail for the night. I think that tomorrow Judge Foulsham will sort it out for you."

Waco smiled as he watched Doc Leroy attending to Fascati's shoulder. If the sheriff and Carelli expected any help from the local judge they were going to get a real big, bad shock in the morning.

"This is an outrage, a deliberate outrage and I will not let the matter rest here. I'm not without friends in the Territorial Capitol I might add."

Mosehan looked at the fat, pompous and well-dressed banker, then at the group of influential citizens grouped round the table of the jail. It was the morning after the arrest, and the town of Calverton was in a state of righteous indignation. The Arizona Rangers were in town, had arrested three of the most respected and prominent citizens and were holding them at the jail. This deputation, led by the banker, was making its second appearance at the jail. The first was not very fruitful for they'd been met at the door by a brusque, drawling young Texas man who refused to release his prisoners or allow anyone to talk with them until his boss, Captain Bertram H. Mosehan, arrived.

The deputation next went to see sheriff, town marshal and judge, but this trio, having conferred the previous night, was not available. The Judge was out making his circuit, the sheriff left to assess taxes at the far end of the county and the town marshal took to his bed with a severe attack of the gripe.

"We came along earlier this morning to order the release

of Mr. Carelli and your man was insulting to us," the owner of the largest store in town went on.

Mosehan hid a grin. He could imagine Waco would be insulting to anyone who tried to take a prisoner from him. The quartet of Rangers here were the tophands of his force and would not allow or submit to anyone taking prisoners from them.

"I heard from my men that you threatened to have them taken from the Rangers," he snapped. "I hire and fire the Rangers and I don't fire them for obeying my orders. I told them to come here, arrest Carelli, Dodd and Spencer. If you've any objections make them to me."

Smethurst, the banker's face turned redder than ever. He was used to respect in large portions from the members of the local law. He started to splutter then cooled down and snapped: "I demand that Mr. Carelli is tried as soon as possible, that way he can clear his name. Will you send one of your men after the judge?"

A tall, slim man stepped from the side door, a man wearing an expensive black suit and with a low-tied gun at his side.

"That won't be necessary, I will be judging the case."

Smethurst looked at the man, thinking he looked like a very successful professional gambler, or an undertaker from a trail-end town. "May I ask who you are?" the banker inquired, very much on his dignity.

"The name is Carmody. I'm the Federal Judge for Arizona Territory. Extortion is a Federal offence. I'll hold the trial tomorrow at noon."

Carelli was standing at the front of his cell, listening to all this. He knew what his chances were if this ever came to a trial and did not like the odds. There was only one slight chance for him.

"How about bail?" he asked.

"Bail?" Carmody turned and looked at the man, listening to the mumble of agreement from the good citizens. He knew that if bail was granted there was little or no chance of the trial ever taking place, for the Mexican border was only two hours steady buckboard drive away. He also realised that a refusal to agree with the bail offer would weaken the already precarious position of the Rangers in this town and would certainly lead to any jury in the town giving a verdict of not guilty, no matter how strong the evidence.

"All right, gentlemen." Carmody looked at the three prisoners. "But in view of the seriousness of the offence I cannot accept a bond of less than seven thousand dollars. Each."

For a moment Carelli was silent; seven thousand dollars was about all the money he could lay his hands on at the moment. He knew his two partners were not so self-sacrificing that they would let him use that money as bail for himself while they remained in prison. They trusted him, but not that much. His eyes went first to the impassive, unsmiling Rangers and the Federal Judge, but there was no chance of getting anything from them. Then he looked at the citizens of the town.

"I can't manage anywhere near that much," he said. "My business was only just getting started and my overheads were high."

Smethurst and the other men looked at each other, then went into a huddle. The merchants of the crowd were getting their goods delivered at less than the standard rate by Carelli, and they liked this. The words, "outrage," "outstanding citizens," and "must help," came through repeated with regularity. Carelli winked at his two partners who were now looking more relieved.

Then at last the banker turned. He looked Judge Car-

mody up and down, gave the Rangers a scowl and finally
said, "If you'll allow, Mr. Carelli, we, your friends, would
like the honour of paying your bail."

"You realise that if the bondees do not appear in court
you forfeit the money, Mr. Smethurst?" Carmody asked.

"Of course I do. I also realise that there is no danger of
that happening. Mr. Carelli and his two partners are first-
class citizens of our town. We trust them implicitly. Don't
we gentlemen?"

There was a chorus of agreement at this and the good
citizens stood waiting for Carelli to be released. However,
Carmody did not give the order and at last they realised
that this was a delivery on payment affair so trooped off to
collect the money.

Mosehan watched the men go, then turned to Billy
Speed. "I got word to Colonel Kosterliski, there should be
a couple of *Rurales* waiting at the border, by the trail.
Head down and check. If there isn't find Don Emilo and
give him this message."

Billy Speed listened to the message, a grin on his face;
he left the office and afork his fast running horse headed
south along the border trail.

Carmody had seen this happen but was not sure just
what it meant. He followed Mosehan and his Rangers into
the side room and sat at the desk. Waco, Doc and Glendon
looked at the leader, waiting for him to speak.

"You look disappointed, Bert," Carmody said.

"Only with the folks here. Look at the way they're acting. Anybody would think my boys were the crooks."

"I couldn't refuse bail."

"I know. You know they'll light out."

Carmody nodded, he was sure that the three men did not
intend to appear for the trial. "There's nothing we can do
about it."

"Was that why you warned the fine public-spirited citizens they'd lose their money?" Waco asked.

"It was."

"They'll lose it, too. That bunch will light out come night. I reckon they'll be gone by midnight."

"They'll head for the border," Doc remarked mildly. "Out of the United States and into Mexico."

"Reckon they'll stick to the main trail?" Waco inquired.

Mosehan looked at the young Texan. There were times when he was sure Waco could read his mind. This was one of the times and Mosehan knew that at least one man guessed what he planned to do.

"Don't you?"

"Sure, they're dudes and they don't travel much. I reckon they'll take their chance on a fast run for the border on a regular trail, rather than going across country."

Carmody looked from one to the other. He'd a lot of faith in Mosehan's capabilities and almost as much in the tall, handsome young Texas boy called Waco. He got the feeling that somehow he'd lost the drift of the conversation, and in this he was not alone, for Doc Leroy and Glendon were looking puzzled.

"What are you two getting at?" the Judge asked.

"Just talking about what Carelli and his pards would do if they jumped their bail and lit out," Mosehan replied. "Which same they don't do, of course, being such pillars of the community."

"What do you aim to do to stop it?" Carmody asked.

"Nothing," Mosehan's voice was mild. "These folks would surely raise a scream if my boys followed Carelli and his bunch: so they aren't going to follow them. The folks'll be real pleased."

"It would be a big loss if they did break their bond."

"The man who put the money up can stand it. Carelli may stand his trial, I don't know."

"But I'd surely bet he doesn't," Waco finished.

The deputation of citizens arrived back with the money for Carelli's bond. They stood by while Judge Carmody counted the notes out and made out a receipt, then to cheers from the crowd outside Carelli, Dodd and Spencer were released.

Carelli stopped at the desk. "I want to say that I hold no hard feelings against the Rangers, they were only doing their job. Mr. Fascati should not have tried to draw his gun although I think he thought it was a hold-up."

The townsmen who were present felt proud of their fellow citizen. He'd been arrested and accused of the Lord only knew what heinous crimes and yet he did not bear the men who arrested him any grudge.

The *Calverton Clarion* came out with a full page editorial condemning the Rangers and demanding an investigation into their methods of operation. The paper was bought out within half-an-hour of publication and the editor decided that he might as well cash in while the boom lasted; so he ran a second edition with substantially the same things in it, but with the added statement that Carelli was the victim of his unscrupulous rivals who'd planted the evidence against him and used the Rangers as their dupes.

Next, the editor went to see Carelli and kept him busy giving a false but highly complimentary story of his life, and how he rose from the poor class in the New York slums to attain his present position in the world. Carelli gave the information although he would much rather have been left to himself and spent the time in getting ready for heading south across the border at midnight.

The next sensation came when the town received news that the Governor himself was coming here. He was on a tour and making a one-night stop at Calverton; this made it awkward for certain of the bail bondsmen as they meant to watch Carelli until trial time. Not, of course, that they did not trust him, but the unscrupulous rivals might kidnap him and get him out of town.

"Man'd say we weren't popular, Cap'n Bert," Waco remarked after reading the third edition of the *Calverton Clarion*. "Wonder what they'll be saying tomorrow?"

Before Mosehan could reply, the jail door opened and Billy Speed came in, a grin on his face that told Mosehan all was well, even before the Ranger gave the news that he'd met Colonel Emilo Kosterliski of the Rurales at the border and all was in hand.

Mosehan sat back in his chair, a look of satisfaction on his face. Carelli was smart, real smart; he'd made this town think he was a benefactor and a real desirable citizen. He'd got everything in his favour here but it was all going to be useless because he did not know of a certain arrangement between Mosehan and Colonel Emilo Kosterliski.

When the Governor arrived, shortly after dark, he was met with a deputation of the leading citizens of the town but took the wind out of their sails right off by introducing Mosehan to them as a friend. He also refused to hear any suggestion that he should intercede on behalf of Carelli.

The influential citizens of the town congregated at the hotel for a dinner and an informal get-together which went on late. Carelli and his two partners made a brief appearance but then left with the excuse that they wanted an early night. The banker watched them go and then once more tried to influence the Governor and Mosehan in favour of Carelli.

Smethurst went along to the hotel to see Carelli early the following morning, and was given the disquieting news that the three men had gone out at midnight and not returned. So Smethurst headed for the Carelli Freight Service depot. The door of the office was thrown open, the safe door standing ajar. Over the floor and scattered about were papers, while in the stove smoked the charred ash of more paper. He frowned as he looked around, then a shadow fell across the floor and he turned to find the tall, blond, handsome young Texan standing in the door.

"You're too late, friend," he said.

"What do you mean, my good man?" Smethurst snapped. He did not like this Arizona Ranger, who after all was only a public servant, nor the way he talked to his betters. He did not show any of the respect Smethurst thought he deserved.

"They've gone, friend, gone like the wind. Took their buggy and lit out. I surely hopes they get back in time for the trial."

For the moment Smethurst looked at the tall young Texan, then around the disordered room. Slowly it sank into his mind what had happened. His face lost all its colour as he thought of the seven thousand he'd personally put up as part of the bond money; if Carelli and the other two were not here for the trial, the money would be forfeit.

"Are you sure they've gone?" he asked hoarsely.

"Sure enough, friend." Waco felt an inner glow of delight now and knew that the good citizens of Calverton were going to regret the way they'd treated the men of the Arizona Rangers. "I came down here to check up on them this morning. The old gent who was their watchman told me he'd seen them take the buggy and pull out at midnight, headed down the south trail."

"The south trail!" Smethurst's voice rose to a strangled scream, "But that leads into Mexico."

"Never thought it led to Canada," Waco answered. "I'd best go back and report to Cap'n Bert."

The words fell on deaf ears as Smethurst turned and headed out of the room fast. He made for the bank and sent hurried messages to all the other men who were Carelli's bondees. They gathered fast and the news they heard brought them on the run to the hotel where they asked for, and were granted, an interview with the Governor.

"I'm sorry, gentlemen." The Governor looked at the men, seeing the guilt in their faces. "You understand that when you stood bail bond for Carelli, Dodd and Spencer you would forfeit your money if they did not show up for the trial?"

"We did, but—but—er—" Smethurst floundered off, at a loss to explain to the man who'd formed them that he thought the Rangers were working for one of Carelli's business rivals.

"I can't change the law any, gentlemen, you realise that. If Carelli is in court all will be well and your faith in him will be justified."

"He's gone into Mexico," a man croaked. "He doesn't mean to come back."

"We don't know that for sure, yet." The Governor felt an unholy joy as he watched these men. "You were so sure of his innocence."

Smethurst could see that the Governor was not in favour of their attitude to the Rangers. He also knew that he was going to eat crow. "Couldn't the Rangers get them back for us?" he asked. "We would give an ample reward."

"If the men are in Mexico my men are helpless." The Governor knew full well that between Bertram Mosehan and Emilo Kosterliski of the *Rurales* was a strictly unofficial arrangement whereby members of the Ranges or the *Guardia Rurale* could either cross the line and pick up their

nationals who'd slipped to the safety of the other side or
call on members of the other force to do it. This, however,
was not an official agreement and nothing could be said of
it in public. He also knew that Carelli and his partners had
been under observation from the moment they climbed into
the buggy and headed south. At the border two members of
the *Guardia Rurale* took over the following with orders
that if Carelli and his men did not stop at Tejanus, a few
miles south of the line, they were to be arrested on some
charge or other and held.

With that cold comfort Smethurst and his men had to be
satisfied. They could see that they'd brought it all on
themselves and there was much recrimination among them
as to who was to blame.

The Governor sat back in his chair after the door had
closed on the deputation and then smiled. From the bedroom where he'd gone at the first sign of the arrival of
Calverton's good citizens, Mosehan strode.

"Well, Bert?" the Governor asked. "Do you know where
they are?"

"In Tejanus most likely. If not they'll be held; Kosterliski's men never fail to obey him."

"Can you get them back again?"

"Not in time for the trial," Mosehan replied, "and I'm
not sure I would if I could. I don't like the way folks in this
damned town have been treating my boys."

"That's a damned immoral outlook, Bert," the Governor
answered, the twinkle in his eyes belying the serious tone
he used. "Unofficially I heartily approve of it. Officially I
must ask you to try to get them back. I won't ask questions
about how they come back."

"Will Judge Carmody delay the trial?" Mosehan glanced
at the clock on the wall. "There's no chance of them being
brought back before trial time."

"We'll see about it. Now get your savages moving."

Mosehan smiled, reached for his hat and walked towards the door.

"They left as soon as Waco reported to me this morning."

Carelli and his partners were not used to the rigours of hunted men and were dog tired when they reached the town of Tejanus in the early hours of the morning. This caused them to head right for bed at the cantina and when they got up again it was well past noon.

In that cantina they found their two men, Tull and Haufman, a pair of big, hard-looking dudes wearing loud check suits and derby hats. The two men showed some surprise at seeing Carelli here and came to their table fast.

"Something wrong, boss?" Tull asked.

"We're in bad trouble," Carelli answered. "The law got on to us and we only got out of town in time."

"What you going to do now?" Tull growled.

"Stay here for a couple of days and see how things go north of the line. I don't think it'll cool down any, so we'll make arrangements to sell out the company then head back East again."

The door of the cantina opened and the two tall, young Texas men came in. Carelli stared at them, anger on his face. "Those two," he hissed. "They're the Rangers who arrested us."

Dodd nodded, then he snapped, "They can't touch us down here."

Carelli knew this without being told, and could see a chance of getting his revenge on the two men. He glanced at Tull and Haufman, then jerked his head to the bar.

Tull came to his feet and lurched forwards across the room; Haufman moved to one side, eyes on the tall handsome boy with the matched brace of guns. He did not give Doc Leroy a second glance, thinking the slim young man would be easy meat.

Waco and Doc stood at the bar, backs to Carelli and his two partners. If they noticed Tull and Haufman they ignored them, ordering their drinks and leaning on the bar, glancing up at the mirror.

Tull halted behind Waco, hand shooting up under his arm and bringing out the short-barrelled gun from his shoulder clip. At the same instant the room broke into wild and sudden activity. Haufman started to whip out his gun to drop Doc Leroy and at the bar two men went into lightning fast and very effective action.

Waco and Doc came round from the bar, spinning like tops and halting, hands already bringing out guns; faster even then Waco, Doc Leroy's ivory-handled gun was crashing and throwing the bullet into Haufman. In echo to the sound, Waco's Colts made a double crash; Tull, caught in the body by the two heavy bullets, was thrown backwards off his feet.

Carelli, Dodd and Spencer rose, staring at the two young Rangers who had once more proved the superiority of western gunsavvy against New York skill.

"All right, Carelli, we've come for you," Waco said.

"This is Mexico, you can't do that to us," Carelli replied, a mocking smile on his face. "It's against international law."

The door of the cantina opened and a tall, hard-faced man stepped in. He wore a grey uniform and on his high-crowned sombrero was the Mexican eagle and snake badge of the *Guardia Rurale*. He raised a hand to stroke the neat beard on his chin and looked Carelli and his two men over.

"I am Colonel Emilo Kosterliski of the *Guardia Rurale*," he announced, his voice the hard clipped and incisive tones of a disciplined martinet, long accustomed to being obeyed instantly. "Have you any passport?"

Carelli shook his head. He was losing some of his colour. "No, but I can—"

"Sergeant!" Kosterliski shouted and the room was swarming with grey uniformed *Rurales*. "Escort these three men back to the border and see they go across."

The ride back to the border was silent and uneventful. Carelli and his two partners were not fools; they knew that they'd fallen into a carefully laid trap. The men in Calverton who'd been their friends, and all for them, would no longer regard them in the same light. They'd lost what might have been a valuable asset in their flight, for they knew Smethurst and the other men would never forgive them for losing the twenty-one thousand dollar bond.

At the rear, riding behind the buggy which carried the bodies of the two killers, Waco and Doc were more than satisfied. They'd done what they came here to do and had helped bring to an end a vicious crooked business.

At the border Mosehan greeted Kosterliski, then gave his attention to the two young Rangers. "How'd it go?"

"Like a stampeded herd," Waco replied. "We couldn't get the two killers alive but we brought them back."

"You know something, Cap'n Bert?" Doc asked.

"What?"

"I don't reckon anybody in Calverton'll be going bail for these three this time."

CASE SEVEN

Gadsby's Conquests

Brad Kinross stood at one side of the body and looked at his friend and fellow Ranger, Waco.

"I killed him. You'd better take me in."

Waco looked down at the body again. The dead man had been very handsome in life, his features the sort which would turn the heads of women anywhere. He wore the uniform of a cavalry captain, the cut of it showing that he was a man with enough money of his own to be able to afford better than the issue clothing of the Army. The bullet which killed him had struck in his right breast and emerged just over his left hip, tearing a big, gaping hole.

For a moment Waco looked down at the still form on the floor, then at the gate in the picket fence around the Kinross house, over the neat flower garden to the house itself. Then he looked along the dusty backstreet they stood in to where a bunch of men were coming this way. Lastly his eyes went up the slope on the other side of the street; on top of that slope was the open range country, mile after mile of grazing land.

The young Texan turned again as the men surged forward, going to his big paint stallion and removing the rope from the saddlehorn. He flipped the noose over one of the picket fence uprights and drew it tight, then turned and spoke to the men as they crowded forward.

"Hold it back there, gents."

The crowd slowed down. They did not know who this tall young Texan man was, but he looked capable of backing any request he made right up to the hilt. In every crowd there was one who couldn't take a gentle hint and needed to be shown: here it was a big, heavy-looking man wearing a store suit.

"Who do you think you are?" he growled and started to move towards the rope.

"The name's Waco, mister. I'm an Arizona Ranger and I don't want folks tromping the sign round that body. All of you keep back until the local law arrives and sees everything."

"Yeah?" The big man started to lift his foot to advance. The foot froze in mid air.

Waco's right-hand gun was in his hand, brought out with a sight-defying speed that told he was a good man with a gun, a man who could not be bluffed or scared by anyone.

"Yeah. Like I said, you stand back. Two of you gents can help me hang this rope around here. Use them two poles in the garden. One of you go and ask the town marshal to come."

The men obeyed, but the big man continued to stand looking at the body, then he asked, "You kill him like you said you would, Brad?"

Before any answer could be made to this, reinforcements to the Ranger group arrived in the shape of Waco's partner, Doc Leroy, and two more members of the force, Pete Glendon and Billy Speed. Doc stepped over the rope and crossed to bend over and examine the body. Glendon

and Billy Speed helped erect the rope in a rough square
around the area. Doc looked at the holes in the soldier's
body, then glanced at a hole low in the gate support. He
looked up at Waco, and the blond youngster nodded,
showing he'd seen and read the message here.

"Tell it, Brad," Waco ordered.

"Nothing to tell. I killed him."

"There's more to it than that," Waco snapped. "You
aren't a killer. Is Sarah to home?"

"No, she's left. I saw her getting on a stage, looked in a
hurry," Doc replied before Kinross could speak.

"She didn't have a thing to do with it!" Kinross spoke
hurriedly. "I killed him. Can't you understand that?"

"When did you kill him?" Doc asked.

"Just before Waco came up. I was looking down at him
when Waco got here."

For a moment Doc looked as if he was going to say
something, then catching a sign from Waco shut his mouth.
Waco looked at the crowd of men standing on the other
side of the rope, then he said, "Pete, take Brad's guns.
He's your prisoner. Hold him while I send word to Cap'n
Bert. Hold him at the house." At that moment three more
Rangers arrived; Waco felt relieved when he saw them, for
what he aimed to do would not meet with the approval of
the local law.

"Ken," he said to one of the men. "Go get that photographer, ask him to take pictures of the body from all sides.
I want them ready as soon as possible. When he's done it,
Dick, you and Sam get the body to the undertaker's and
bring me the jacket back here."

The other men accepted Waco's orders without ques-
tion. In the Rangers there was only one leader, Captain
Mosehan himself, but the other men were willing to take
Waco's orders for they knew he would have a good reason

for everything he did. The crowd of townsmen stood around, talking amongst themselves but making no attempt either to help or hinder the Rangers. They showed some interest when the town marshal arrived, but he was one of the lawmen who regarded the Rangers as being an efficient and capable force and was willing to leave the investigation of the shooting in their hands: until he heard from the big man that Brad Kinross had confessed to the killing.

"You said you'd kill him if he came round here again Brad," Hardman, the marshal, growled. "I'm going to take you in."

Hardman met Waco's eyes for a moment, then looked away. He was the town law and head of Grand Rock's three-man police force, but he was only a minor official when compared with the Territorial Rangers. He could not see any way he could take the prisoner from the Rangers even by violence, for they were all men picked for, among other things, skill with their guns.

Waco stepped over the rope and swung afork the big paint, riding to the town's main street. He swung down from the horse and was leading it into the livery barn when a woman came out and crashed into him. She staggered back, dropping the double-barrelled gun from under her arm.

"Sorry, ma'am," Waco said, bending and picking the gun up.

"It was my fault, young man."

The woman was a beauty; tall, with a figure that caught the eye. She would be in her early forties, he guessed, but she was possessed of that mature beauty only a few women ever attain. There was a look about her, a lordly conde-scension, a kind of aloof disdain which said she was some-one to be reckoned with. Her clothes were very expensive; the riding habit she wore and the J. B. stetson hat on her red hair. The gun was expensive, too, a finely chased piece which had cost plenty.

Before Waco could say another word the woman swept by him and along the street. He took the paint into the barn and arranged for a couple of loose boxes; one for his horse and one for Doc's big black stallion. The old-timer who was working at the barn grinned at him, "See you met the Colonel?" he said.

"Who?" Waco inquired.

"The Colonel, Mrs. Stacey, she's the one who runs the 19th Cavalry up to the fort. Real lady, might be too high-handed for some but she's always treated me good."

Waco unsaddled the big horse and left his gear with the owner of the barn pending his return. He walked out on to the street and headed for the telegraph office; inside he sent a message to his boss. It was half-an-hour before the reply came back, but when it did, Waco was more than satisfied with it. Brad Kinross was lucky. He couldn't have asked for better luck than having all the Rangers gathering in his home town of Grand Rock to have a group photograph taken; that ensured him twelve real good, loyal friends who would back him to the hilt. Yet he'd got more than just that piece of luck.

The telegraph reached Mosehan while he was with the Governor of Arizona Territory and that gentleman gave the signature to any action the Rangers felt they should take. Waco was relieved at this for he was going to tread on a whole lot of toes before this thing was over.

Just as he reached the street he stopped dead; opposite was the Wells Fargo office. He crossed the street and entered, asking a couple of questions of the agent, then came out. Billy Speed was just leading his own and Glendon's horses towards the livery barn and Waco crossed to stop him.

"Get afork your horse; take Pete's with you and go after the stage to Calverton," he said. "It don't make any speed and you should catch up with it easy. Tell Sarah Kinross to come back here." He gave the thin, cheerful looking Ranger a message for the girl and watched Bill vault afork his horse and head off out of town, then returned to the Kinross place.

The county sheriff's department was on hand when he arrived, represented by the deputy who stayed in Grand Rock all the time. He looked at Waco, "You Waco?"

"The only one, friend."

"I want Kinross."

"You can't have him," Waco replied and took out the telegraph message form, holding it for the deputy to read.

The deputy read, "Waco. Hold on authority of Governor, Ranger Kinross, pending my arrival to investigate. Mosehan."

"Well?"

"You can see it for yourself, friend. Captain Mosehan's told me to hold him and hold him she is."

The deputy frowned; he was not sure exactly what rights he had in the matter but wasn't going against the Governor of Arizona. He turned on his heel and headed for the telegraph office to send to the county seat for instructions as to what he should do now.

Waco went into the house. The body was removed as he'd said and Glendon was seated with Kinross; Doc stood looking out of the window. Kinross sat at the table, head resting on his hands. He looked up at Waco, his face showing the deep strain he was under.

Waco sat at the table, and his voice was hard and unfriendly as he asked, "Who was he and what happened?"

"His name was Gadsby. Dane Gadsby, he's a Captain of the 19th up there at the fort. I killed him."

"Why, and why'd you threaten to kill him?"

"He kept pestering Sarah. Wouldn't leave her alone. I told him to stay clear of her and he got two of his men to try and beat me up. I managed to fix them and I went to see him in the saloon; warned him that if he came near our place again I'd kill him."

Waco was watching his friend's face all the time, knowing that Brad Kinross was hiding something. "That sounds a mite hard, Brad. Sarah's a real pretty gal and it's only natural for a man to go after a nice, pretty gal. I've seen you chase a couple in your time."

"That depends on how a man chases them. You know that I was just after fun. Gadsby wasn't. I learned a whole lot about him before I made my move. He's been thrown out of every command he's been with for the same thing. I got to know his striker and he told me all about how his boss keeps a book with photographs and all the details about the girls he's been with. Calls it Gadsby's Conquests. The striker was pretty drunk and he told me Gadsby told him that he aimed to add Sarah to his list. That was why I told him to stay away from her."

"How about Sarah, did she ever encourage him any?"

Kinross threw back his chair and came to his feet, fist clenched, then slowly he relaxed, for Waco never moved. "You know Sarah. Since maw and paw died we've been close together. No, Sarah danced a couple of times with him, but you know she's been going steady with young Tom McCall. She wanted no part of Gadsby, but he took to hanging about outside the house, that was when I cut in. I didn't want him doing it when I was out on a Ranger chore."

"Trouble, Waco," Doc said, from the window. "We've got the Army here now."

Waco rose and joined his friend. A tall, hard-looking Colonel, a Major and a squad of troopers under a sergeant were approaching the gate. The Colonel came through and followed by the Major strode up to the house door. Waco waited until the knock came then went to it.

"Kinross?" the Colonel asked as Waco opened the door and stepped out, closing it behind him again.

"Nope, Colonel. Waco, Arizona Rangers."

"Where is Kinross?"

"Inside."

"I'm Colonel Stacey of the 19th Cavalry. Kinross killed one of my officers. I want him."

"He's my prisoner."

Stacey looked at this young-looking Texan, finding eyes that met his own; met and did not flinch from the gaze which cowed soldiers. Then slowly the Colonel looked down at the matched guns in Waco's holsters. Stacey could read the signs and knew that here was a man who could handle those same guns.

"He murdered a member of the United States Cavalry," Stacey barked. "I've come personally to arrest him."

"I'm real sorry, Colonel. My orders from our leader, Cap'n Mosehan, is to hold Brad until he comes here to take charge of the investigations." Waco held out the telegraph message form. "That's my authority, Colonel."

Stacey ignored the telegraph form, his eyes hard. "I want that man. Do you intend to stop me taking him?"

"If I have to."

"You'd fight United States soldiers to hold onto a murderer?"

"Like I said, Colonel. He's my prisoner. I'd fight the devil himself before I'd let him take a prisoner from me. And Brad hasn't been convicted by court yet, so he isn't proved a murderer."

For a time the two faced each other, the older man's hard eyes softening as he realised that here was a young

man doing his duty and standing firm in his orders in a way
many a trained soldier would admire.

"You couldn't fight off all my regiment," Stacey finally
remarked.

"No, Colonel, but happen you try to take my prisoner
I'm surely going to make me a good try."

"He won't escape?" the Major asked.

"If it ever comes that he needs trying, Brad'll be here
for the same trial," Waco answered. "I've got my orders,
gentlemen, and I surely aims to follow them right through
till the last card's played."

Stacey's face still showed his respect for the young
Texan. He turned on his heel and started towards the gate.
He halted and looked back. "I'd like to see both you and
your leader when he arrives. Come to my house up by the
fort."

"We'll do that, Colonel," Waco answered. He remained
at the door until the Colonel had walked away and the
troopers were marched back towards the fort, then went
into the house again.

One of the other Rangers came back. He'd been with
the photographer and in his hand he carried three large
prints of the body, showing how it lay in comparison to the
fence. Glendon took the photographs and looked at them.
They were not very clear prints but showed all that was
necessary.

"Not a bad idea, this, Waco," he said.

"Got its uses," Waco agreed.

"You just think of it?"

"Nope, met a detective from the Chicago police, he told
me they sometimes use photographs in cases like this."

"It important?"

"Sure, Pete. These pictures show just how Gadsby was
lying."

The other two Rangers came back at that moment, bringing the coat Gadsby was wearing when he died. Waco sent one of them to fetch the deputy sheriff, the marshal and the judge. Then he looked up the slope and said, "Feel like taking a walk, Pete?"

Glendon showed some surprise at this, for Waco was a cowhand born and raised, and would never walk when he could ride. However, Glendon followed the young man up the slope, and on top he watched Waco looking for something. Glendon was no mean hand at following tracks or reading the marks left on the ground, and saw the marks in the short grass just an instant after Waco. From the way the grass was crushed both read that someone had walked this way, then knelt at the top of the rim, looking down at the house below, right at the spot where Gadsby stood when he was killed.

The tracks led for a short distance to a mesquite scrub where a horse had been tethered for a short time. From there on there were no more footprints, only the marks the horse left. Waco and Glendon looked at each other for a time, then Glendon asked:

"What do you make of it all, boy?"

"Could be important, might be nothing. We don't have time to try and trail the hoss right now."

"I'll follow them if you like," Glendon suggested, for he, too, saw the marshal and the two other men coming towards the house.

"Do that," Waco answered and turned to hurry down the slope.

The Judge was a portly, tanned man; a keen outdoors man who would rather take a day's hunting than a trial. He was also honest, scrupulously fair and impartial. He looked as Waco came down the slope and advanced to meet them.

"I can't say I like your high-handed way of doing things, Ranger," he said.

"Would the marshal have turned one of his deputies over to me, had he been in my place, Judge?" Waco replied. "I held on to Brad for the same reason. Then when I got my orders from Cap'n Mosehan I surely couldn't just pull out and disobey them."

"I see your point, now, why did you want us to come here?"

"To prove something to you. I want to clear Brad Kinross and his sister of the killing."

"Nobody blames Brad for killing Gadsby," the marshal growled. "If a man like that'd been after my daughter or sister I'd have done the same."

"Brad didn't kill Gadsby. He said he did because he thought Sarah had killed him. Sarah thought Brad'd done it and she ran out. Took a stage out of town. I don't know why she ran unless it was to make everyone think she'd done the killing and clear Brad."

"All right, but shouldn't it be done in a courtroom?"

"No, Judge, it shouldn't," Waco replied. "Brad is an Arizona Ranger. If he goes to court, all the bunch who are after Cap'n Mosehan and getting the Rangers disbanded will have something to get their teeth into. They'll want to see him convicted, innocent or guilty, and they'll swear we rigged the evidence if we get him off. I want to prove to you that Brad couldn't have done the killing and he doesn't need to stand trial for it."

The other Rangers came from the house. Brad Kinross looked at Waco with pleading in his eyes. Waco, however, was looking over the other men, then said to one of the Rangers, "Tom, you look about the same height as Gadsby. Put his coat on."

The Ranger took the blood-covered coat and without a

word slipped it on; it was a fair fit and he stood waiting for Waco's next orders. The young Texan looked at the others then stepped forward, handing the Judge his photographs of the body.

"Gadsby was stood here," Waco said, putting the other Ranger in position. "I think he was facing with his left to the house, like this." Waco turned the other man round into position. "Now that bullet hit here," Waco indicated the small hole in the right breast, then pointed to the large tear at the left side. "And came out down here, ending in the gatepost, here. Any of you gents got a piece of string on you?"

"Here you are, boy," the Judge pulled a long length of string from his pocket, handing it over. He was looking more interested now, although the marshal and the deputy were obviously puzzled by all this.

"Hold this end on the bullet hole in the post, Brad," Waco ordered, and Kinross, still looking puzzled, did so. "Now gents, bullets do strange things, but they always go through the air in near enough a straight line," Waco went on, running the line through his hands and up to the bullet hole at the left side, then across the body to the other hole and moving back, keeping the cord in a straight line. Before he'd taken many steps back his arms were stretched above his head and pointing the cord towards the top of the slope.

For a moment none of the men spoke, then the marshal growled, "Gadsby could have been stood the other way round."

"And the bullet went down, through the post without making a mark on the other side; flew round Gadsby's body, down in the right and out again?" Waco's contempt was obvious to see.

The Judge studied the situation, then looked up at the

top of the rim and asked, "What did you find up there?"

"Somebody knelt there, likely the killer. Couldn't tell much from the sign, it wasn't clear enough to make out bootshape or anything, being on short grass. But from the length of the stride I made it smaller than Brad and taller than Sarah."

"About five foot seven or eight them?" the Judge inquired; he'd hunted often enough to know something about the reading of sign.

"About that," Waco agreed. "Brad, go up to the house and get a saw or a hammer and chisel, the bullet's still in there and I want it out."

The other men stood around, silent and all busy with their own thoughts as the Rangers worked carefully to dig out the bullet which had killed Captain Gadsby. It took only a short time and Brad Kinross, his face relaxed and showing relief, held out a piece of lead. Apart from some mushrooming of the head the bullet was intact and from one glance is was obviously not fired from a revolver.

"Looks like a rifle bullet," the marshal said.

"That figgers," the Judge growled. "I never saw a revolver that'd carry from the top of that rim there, go clear through a man and bury into a wood post. What sort of rifle do you have, Brad?"

"A Winchester Centennial, but it's in the gunsmith's and has been for three days now. There's a couple of Winchester 73s in the house and a Ballard."

"That lets you out then." The Judge looked relieved. "This came from a high-powered rifle. A .45.70 at least."

"That's the Army calibre," the deputy sheriff remarked.

"Sure, but that bunch there are cavalry. They use the Springfield carbine and that wouldn't have the range," Waco pointed out, then he looked at Brad. "Now why in hell's name did you say you'd shot him?"

"I was coming back from town when I thought I heard a shot. I came round the corner there and saw Sarah standing looking down at Gadsby. Then she looked up and saw me; she turned and ran back into the house. I thought she'd done it."

"Had you got your gun in your hand when you came round the corner?" Waco asked.

"Sure, I didn't know what I might run into and wasn't taking any chances."

"So Sarah thought you'd killed him and you thought she'd done it. She ran out the back of the house, went to the stage depot and lit out of town so folk would blame her, you stayed here and tried to say you'd done it."

Brad Kinross looked at the other men around him. He'd known the Judge, the marshal and the deputy sheriff most of his life and read friendship and belief in their faces.

"Never thought you'd done it at all, Brad," the marshal stated. "I thought I should be the one to hold you though."

At that moment, Billy Speed and a pretty, red-haired girl came round the corner riding their horses at a good speed. The girl slid down from her horse and ran up to Brad, throwing her arms round his neck and kissing him.

"Take her up to the house, Brad," Waco suggested. "Judge, I'd like you to come along and see the Colonel, and explain to him what you've just seen."

"Certainly I'll come. The sooner this thing is cleared up the better. Who did kill Gadsby?"

"That I don't know," Waco replied.

"I'd take it as a favour if you'd stay on and try to find out. From what I've just seen of you, I think you could."

The Judge and Waco walked side by side on to Grand Rock's main street and saw Pete Glendon coming towards them. He stopped and told Waco that the tracks of the horse had ended upon the main trail and he'd not been able to follow them any more, nor get any clear imprint on which he might be able to locate the horse. Waco was expecting this and was not unduly bothered about it. There might, or might not, be a chance of finding the man who'd killed Gadsby, but with Brad Kinross in the clear, Waco was not too worried; it now came under the jurisdiction of the local law or the Army.

The Judge led the way, not to the fort but to a fair-sized, white painted, house near the gates. On the post-box at the end of the path leading to the door was painted, "Col. Elvin J. T. Stacey, 19th United States Cavalry."

Knocking on the door the Judge remarked, "More likely to find the Colonel here than at the fort at this time of the day."

The door was opened by a large, fat and smiling negress who apparently knew the Judge, for she stepped aside, "Come in, Judge, come right on in."

The Judge and Waco entered the hall and were taken to the sitting room, waved inside and left. The room interested Waco, it reminded him of Ole Devil Hardin's study back in the Rio Hondo country of Texas. Both were alike in the air of masculine comfort and lack of feminine frills. The walls were decorated with paintings of battle scenes and animal heads. On the floor was a buffalo hide rug which was met by the skin of a large silver top grizzly. Over the fireplace a pair of crossed guidons with holes in them which might have been caused by hostile bullets. Waco's eyes went to the stand of arms in the corner; there was a fine looking Springfield officer's model rifle, a couple of Winchesters, a Sharps and four double-barrelled guns. On a small table near where Waco was standing a copy of the *Army and Navy Journal* lay, open in the centre of the correspondence page. Waco was just about to pick it up and read the letter when the door at the other end of the room opened and a tall, red haired, beautiful woman came in. Although she now wore a stylish, though rather severe-looking dress instead of a riding habit Waco recognised her.

"Afternoon, Laura," the Judge said, holding out his hand. "We came round to see Elvin but he's still across at the fort."

"Yes," the woman's voice was cool, impersonal and cultured. "He's rather busy arranging for Dane Gadsby's funeral." Her eyes flickered at Waco, leaving him feeling very young and inexperienced. "I think we've met somewhere."

"Came together'd be a better way of putting it, ma'am," Waco replied.

"Of course. You're the young man I bumped into outside the livery barn. I'm sorry about that. I was rather engrossed and didn't see you coming."

"This's one of the Arizona Rangers; Waco's his name," the Judge remarked. "He's in charge of investigating Gadsby's death."

"Really, I expected a much older man. So you are the one who refused to hand over his prisoner to my husband?"

"Yes, ma'am. I'm surely sorry but I had my orders—"

"And you carried them out. Never apologise for doing your duty, young man. My husband was rather impressed by your action. He thinks you'd make a good soldier."

"Not unless I rode under the Stars and Bars, ma'am."

The woman smiled, her face lighting up as she looked at him. She held out her hand to him, her grip firm and strong. Somehow, even though she was a really beautiful woman, Waco did not regard her as such. He felt that she would never really be at home in the company of other women but would prefer to be around men.

"What did you wish to see Elvin about, Charles?"

"Like we said, Gadsby's killing, ma'am," Waco put in, speaking bluntly and watching her face all the time.

"A tragic ending to a career. One of your men is under suspicion of the killing, isn't he?"

"Yes, ma'am, that's why I want to see your husband."

"What could he do to help you?"

"Gadsby was one of his men and I don't know how the Army stand together. I'd like him to place the town off limits until we've finished with the matter. It'll save some trouble and friction with the local folks," Waco replied. "Remember when an officer of the 14th Infantry got killed in a gunfight in Fort Worth. The troopers in town got into fights and trouble—"

"They were only infantry," Laura Stacey answered. "Not the 19th Cavalry. We've quite a tradition behind us and one of the things the 19th can say is that we've never made trouble for any civilians."

"You know some about the regiment, ma'am?" Waco asked, glancing at the nearest picture which depicted a cavalry charge on a Confederate artillery battery.

"I should, my father organised and commanded it. That is the 19th's charge on the 2nd Virginia Artillery at the battle of Shell Creek. It was that charge which saved the day and brought victory out of what could easily have been defeat."

"Sounds like you know the regiment real well, ma'am."

"Know it. Laura is the 19th Cavalry," the Judge put in. "I bet she can tell you every action they ever fought in and damned near every man who ever served with the regiment since it started."

"You exaggerate, Charles." Laura Stacey showed some pride at the Judge's words. "I have been with the 19th, except when they were in the field, ever since it was formed. We have a great tradition, Ranger. That is what makes a truly great regiment, tradition, honour—"

"And no scandal."

Laura Stacey looked at the Judge, and there was annoyance in her eyes. "There has never been any breath of scandal attached to the 19th Cavalry and never will."

At that moment the Negro maid looked in and asked Laura to go to the kitchen with her to check over some supplies which had just arrived form the local store. The Judge watched Laura sweep from the room and then turned back to Waco, and smiling, said:

"She's a great one for the regiment, Laura is." He took a seat in one of the chairs. "Like she says, she was born to it. They reckon the only reason she married Stacey was because he was the one most likely to get the promotion to Colonel. She shoved him on to the top. Only time you'll ever see her rattled is if there's something wrong with the regiment."

Waco went to the small table and took up the *Army and Navy Journal*. He'd often read it in Texas and found the letters the most interesting part. One caught his eye straight away.

"Better than Singleshot.

"Sirs,

"I would like to take up the issue of singleshot or repeating rifles." Waco grinned, the controversy over whether the Army should be issued with repeating or singleshot arms was one which had raged since before the Civil War. The official policy being that a singleshot arm was stronger, more reliable and that a repeater would need too much time spent in keeping it clean, and would also tend to make the user waste ammunition. "I understand the official policy and would like to suggest that if no repeating arm is found which is satisfactory then a double-barrelled rifle would be the answer. I have recently purchased such a rifle from Colt. In calibre it is .45.70. It is as easy to care for and far easier to reload than the Springfield carbine. Nor in the time I have used it have I ever had a cartridge case jam in the breech. Had George Custer's command been armed with double-barrelled rifles at the Battle of Little Bighorn things might have come far different."

Waco read through the letter and, at the end, the signature of the sender. He was a thoughtful young man as he glanced at the stand of arms in the corner. Turning, he said, "I'd best go and see if Cap'n Mosehan's arrived yet. If he's here I'll fetch him round."

The Judge showed Waco out and returned to the sitting room. He did not see the young man head, not for the Kinross place, but for the far side of the fort where, in a dry-wash, the cavalry had fixed up a target range. On reaching this, Waco grubbed around until he found what he was looking for. He slipped the thing into his pocket and headed for town, still not going to the Kinross house, but to the livery barn.

The old timer who'd been there when Waco brought his horse in was still on duty. He came across and watched as Waco stroked the neck of the big paint.

"Fine hoss, Ranger," he said.

That gave Waco the chance he'd been waiting for. Livery barn staff were as talkative as barbers and the old man was full of the news and views of the town. He tried to pump Waco about the killing and appeared to think that even if Brad Kinross shot Gadsby he was only doing something which should have been done much sooner.

Waco was a capable talker, one who knew how to steer a conversation any way he wanted it to go without arousing the other's suspicions. He brought the talk round to guns, then shooting for sport.

"Any chance of getting some bird shooting round here, Colonel?" he asked.

"You mean with a scatter gun?"

"Why sure, I did some wing shooting back in Texas and reckon it's real good for keeping the sighting eye in. Ain't seed much out here to shoot though."

"There's plenty on the range, prairie chicken and turkey for two. You saw Mrs. Stacey this morning. She goes out most days with a shotgun after birds. Today was the first time she didn't bring any back. Must have been them new-fangled sights on the gun she'd got with her."

"Sights. I thought all shotguns had sights."

"These were rifle sights, set on the wrist of the stock. Pity, it was a real, fine double-barrelled gun. Shouldn't never have tried rifle sights on it."

"Could you tell that gun again?" Waco asked, his voice showing none of the excitement he felt. "See, I'm borrowing a gun from the Colonel and I surely don't want that one."

The old-timer snorted. "Surely I could tell it again. Real new-looking gun, fine worked too, fancy checkered grip. Only that sight on the wrist spoils it."

"I'll remember that, Colonel. I'd best get round to see Brad. See you around, Colonel."

Waco went round to the Kinross house as fast as he could make it. One of the other Rangers was leading a steaming, sweating horse. He jerked his thumb to the house and remarked, "Cap'n Bert's there and waiting for you."

Going up the path Waco knocked on the door and entered. Mosehan was seated at the table, his face showing the strain of riding a four-horse relay from Tucson, covering ground fast to get here. He looked up at Waco, then at Brad Kinross and Doc Leroy who were seated in the room.

"What do you know, Waco?" Mosehan asked.

"Tell you on the way to see a man," Waco replied. "If you feel like walking, Cap'n. You're not getting any younger."

"Younger," Mosehan snorted. "What do you think I am, old?"

They walked through the streets and Waco told Mosehan all he suspected as they walked. At the Stacey house the coloured maid let them in an showed them to the sitting room again. Colonel Stacey, his wife and the Judge were seated round the table; the Colonel rose as Waco came in. Stacey was cordial to Waco and polite when the young Texan introduced Mosehan.

"What do you intend doing about that man of yours, Mosehan?" Stacey asked.

"Nothing. Brad is innocent."

Stacey looked at Mosehan for a time, then asked, "Isn't that for a court to decide?"

"Not unless the Judge wants the town in trouble for false arrest. Waco here has proved Kinross' innocence; right, Judge?"

"That's right. I'll show you what he means if you want to come down there and see for yourself, Elvin."

"Who did the killing then?" Stacey snapped. "Or don't you know?"

"The boy here thinks he knows," Mosehan answered. "He's one of my best men, the one who caught Massey after he'd tried to murder Chief Victorio. Reckon he'd best tell you what he told me on the way here."

Stacey looked at Waco with fresh respect; he'd heard of the murder attempt on the life of the old Apache chief, Victorio, when the chief came in to sign the peace treaty. He glanced at his wife, who sat erect in her chair, face showing no expression at all, but her hands clenched together.

"Brad Kinross didn't kill Gadsby. I proved that to the Judge and I'll go and prove it to you, Colonel. Brad confessed because he thought Sarah, his sister, killed him. Sarah thought Brad'd done it and she took a stage out of town. That made Brad sure she'd done it. She went because she thought the suspicion would fall on her rather than him. What neither knew was that Gadsby was dead before either of them came near him. I'm going to talk plain, Colonel, with all respect to Mrs. Stacey, and I'm going to say things that neither of you is going to like, but they are true and need to be said. So let the cards fall as they're played. One of my friends is in trouble. This thing could ruin all Cap'n Mosehan's worked for, it will give the bunch who hate the Rangers and want to get rid of them something to work on. I'm not having a killing hanging over Brad Kinross."

"We'll accept that," Stacey answered. "Carry on, no matter how unpleasant."

"First, Gadsby was a woman-chasing, no-good trouble causer and to hell with speaking well of the dead. He'd been thrown out of every Army job he held for the same thing. He wasn't just a woman chaser, he was a vicious, callous brute who treated women worse than dogs. You all know about Gadsby's Conquests, how he flaunted them before the other members of his mess. This time the girl he chose for his conquest was sensible enough to get out before it was too late. That hurt his vanity and he started to chase her. She'd got a brother who was tough, capable and handy. He told Gadsby to stay away from her and Gadsby sent two troopers to work Brad over. That was why Brad Kinross said he'd kill Gadsby if he didn't stay away from Sarah."

"You're making a good case for your friend to have killed Gadsby, Ranger," Stacey put in. "I don't know where you heard so much about Gadsby, and I'm not going to admit it is true."

"We'll pass that, Colonel, you know what is true and what isn't. Sure, I've made a good case for Brad to have killed Gadsby. But Brad isn't the sort who'd need to drop a man in cold blood. He's good with a gun and I mean good. Colonel, Brad was fast enough to let Gadsby start lifting his gun, then still kill him before he could line it. Why'd Brad lay for Gadsby with a rifle, down him and risk being caught for murder when he could take Gadsby in a fair fight, or what'd pass for a fair fight, and kill him without giving the law a chance to touch him?"

"You say a rifle. How did you know that?"

"The bullet went right through Gadsby and buried into the gatepost. From the angle it went, the bullet must have come from a rifle. A revolver, fired at the range that bullet came from, wouldn't have been powerful enough to do it."

"Then if your friend didn't kill Gadsby, who did?"

"Somebody who hated Gadsby for what he was. Who knew the kind of man he was and that he would bring trouble to everyone round him and ruin the good name of the regiment by his actions. Someone with a .45.70 rifle; not a carbine, but a rifle."

"There is no proof of any of that, Ranger," Laura Stacey spoke for the first time. Her tones were even but there was a slight tremor in them.

"I can get it, ma'am. The old gent at the livery barn and I both saw that Colt double-barrelled rifle you'd taken with you this morning. Saw the backsight on the wrist."

Stacey came to his feet, angry words coming from his lips, but his wife laid a hand on his sleeve. "I carried a double-barrelled gun, I often do, old Wilson at the livery barn knows that. I often give him the birds I bring back."

"That's why he noticed the gun, ma'am. You didn't bring any back today," Waco replied, dipping his hand into his pocket and dropping a cartridge case on the table. "I found this where you knelt and lined the rifle on Gadsby."

"I didn't unload the gun there!"

Stacey and the other men were all on their feet, the Colonel's face twisted in rage, his body tensing to hurl at this young man who'd come into his home and accused his wife of murdering a man. Then he realised what Laura's words meant. He looked at his wife. She stood there, hands at her sides, head held erect, face showing no expression now she'd made that slip.

"All right, Ranger, I killed Gadsby," she said. Through the blur in front of her eyes she saw her husband's haggard face. "I'm sorry, Elvin. From the start I warned you what kind of man he was. His reputation came ahead of him and I could see that he would bring a scandal on the regiment. He was obsessed with one idea: getting Sarah Kinross amongst his conquests. He meant to do it any way he could. I didn't mean to kill him this morning and I'd taken the Colt rifle out to try and shoot a pronghorn buck I'd seen. I was on the way back along the rim behind the Kinross house when I saw Gadsby coming up. I knew that he was going to make some trouble and that what he was doing would ruin the regiment. I couldn't let him do it."

"So you shot him, ma'am," Waco said softly.

"I shot him. My father made this regiment; made it and kept its tradition for chivalry and honour. Gadsby was ruining all that he stood for, so I shot him down like I would a mad dog. I wouldn't have let your friend stand trial for the murder, Ranger. I meant to write a letter and leave it for the town marshal and go East. Now it is out in the open and I'm glad it is."

"What do you aim to do, Ranger?" Stacey asked, his voice hoarse as he put his arm round the shoulders of his wife.

"That depends on Cap'n Mosehan. I want to see Brad cleared of the killing. The Arizona Rangers haven't been formed long but we've got a tradition ourselves. A tradition for honesty, loyalty to each other and to Cap'n Bert. It won't do the Rangers any good if word gets out that one of our men is suspected of murder. I just want to see him cleared."

And he will be, I promise you that," Laura Stacey answered. "Judge, I and I alone killed Gadsby; Brad and Sarah Kinross were in no way implicated."

Waco took up his hat, looked at Mosehan and then said, "I'm sorry about having to do this, ma'am. If there is anything I can do to help—"

"Nothing, thanks, Ranger." It was Stacey who answered, for the first time in his life taking charge of his wife's affairs. "You did your duty as you saw it, as Laura did hers. There is no need to apologise for that."

Waco left the house and went to the gate. He stood there for a time, then a hand fell on his shoulder. He turned and looked at Mosehan who stood just behind him. For a moment neither of them spoke, then the Ranger Captain gently patted the broad shoulder.

"What'll happen to her, Captain?"

"She'll be tried; after that, *quien sabe*?"

They walked together towards Brad Kinross' home where the rest of their men would be waiting for them, all eager to hear their news.

CASE EIGHT

One of Dusty's Guns

The sound of the fight brought Waco on the run round the rear of the silent and deserted building in Backsight. In the dim half light he saw a young man struggling with two others, while a third smashed a revolver into the wall of the building. Waco did not wait to see or hear what it was all about; he was always ready to pitch in and help against odds of three to one, more so when even in the dull light of the Arizona night he recognised a fellow lawman in trouble.

Catching one of the pair Waco swung him round and smashed a right into him, throwing him backwards. The other man let loose and drove his fist hard into the side of Waco's face, knocking him into the wall. The young Texan ducked as the third man brought the gun slashing round at him. He heard the weapon crash into the woodwork over his head; the base pin burst and the chamber came out of its opening and fell to the ground. Waco's fist smashed into the man's stomach, his other fist coming round to land full on the side of the man's ear.

Waco heard a hissing sound. He tried to duck under the gun barrel he knew was coming, but was too late. The expensive J. B. Stetson had saved him for the worst of the blow, but he was dropped to the ground, his head spinning.

"Get out of here," a voice yelled.

Through the spinning and roaring in his head Waco heard another thud and then the sound of running feet as his attackers departed fast. He pushed himself up onto his hands and knees, shaking his head to clear it. He got to his feet; the man he'd come to save was also down, holding his head and groaning in agony.

Taking his right-hand gun from the holster Waco fired two shots into the air, then tried to guess which way the three men had gone. He shoved the gun away and leaned against the wall. A few moments later he saw lanterns and two men came running up.

"What've you been doing, boy?"

Waco felt relieved to see his partner, Doc Leroy, carrying one of the lanterns, and in the light it gave recognised the man he'd come to save. Waco had guessed it was the Backsight deputy town marshal, Tommy Melveny, and now knew he was right.

"You tell him, Tommy. I just happened by, saw you and came to help."

Tommy Melveny got to his feet, looking round dazedly, his eyes going to the two Arizona Rangers and to the huge bulk of Biscuits Randle, the marshal. Then he saw the ruined gun lying on the ground and went to it, picking it up. He looked at the space where the chamber should be, then at the broken base pin.

"This is my gun!" he gasped.

"Sure," Waco agreed. "What happened, Tommy?"

"My gun, they've bust my gun!" Tommy Melveny did not appear to know what Waco was saying to him.

"Who did it and why?"

It took some seconds for the words to sink into

Tommy's mind, he was staring down at the broken gun. Even so, he did not say anything and Biscuits growled, "What happened here?"

"Found three hombres working Tommy over and came to help him," Waco replied. "One of them pistolwhipped me and then they lit out."

"Lucky you'd got your hat on, you might have damaged his gun," Doc said dryly. "Let's get back to the office and I'll do what I can for that cut on your face, Tommy."

Tommy still had not spoken by the time they got back to the one-storey adobe building which housed the Backsight jail, the offices of the Town Marshal and the County Sheriff. In the marshal's office Doc found the cut on Tommy's face was more bloody than dangerous so stood back. Waco leaned on the desk and asked:

"Who did it, Tommy?"

"I don't know for sure. There were three of them and that's all I know. They jumped me as I made my rounds, dragged me back there. Two of them held me while the other started to smash my gun. He bust up my gun."

"You can get another," Doc remarked cheerfully. "Or does sparking Molly Howard keep you short of cash?"

"I can't get another gun like this one," Tommy indicated the battered gun on the desk top. "It belonged to Bad Bill Longley. That's why I was so good with it."

"That's loco," Waco put in. "Even if it was one of Bad Bill's guns, which I can't see, it wouldn't make any difference to you or to the way you handle it."

"That's where you're wrong, Waco," Tommy sounded deadly serious. "The man I bought it off was a Texan who'd ridden with Longley. He took the grip off and showed me where Longley scratched his name on it. You remember, Biscuits?"

"Sure," Biscuits agreed. "It wasn't until after you

bought that gun that you showed how well you could use one."

Waco frowned; he knew that the chances of this gun ever actually having belonged to the Mill Creek terror, Bad Bill Longley, were not great. He also knew that just thinking the gun belonged to Longley gave Tommy added confidence.

"You'll have to get another gun and make some practice with it," Waco remarked.

"I won't have time. Check Thompson's coming to town tomorrow, looking for me," there was a touch of panic in Tommy's voice. "That must have been his pards who bust the gun."

"Who's Check Thompson?" Doc inquired.

"A gunhand, worked for one of the outfits just below the county line," Biscuits replied. "He came up here and got likkered. Took to shooting the lights out at the Alamo and Tommy buffaloed him, throwed him in jail. When he came out he went home but he said he'd be back."

"And last week I heard he was coming back; he'll be here about noon tomorrow."

There was something very close to fear in Tommy's eyes. Watching, Waco could see it and read it. The young deputy was brave enough, yet he held to the idea that it was owning Longley's gun which had made him what he was. Waco knew that Tommy was the most rare of gunfighters, a natural. He had the balance, sense of timing and the uncanny eye that enabled him to draw and shoot fast; accurate, yet without needing to keep in practice.

"You'll just have to get another gun then," Waco suggested.

"Where can I get another of Longley's guns?" Tommy answered, then rose and left the room.

Biscuits looked at the other two men. He was no gunfighter and rarely if ever even wore a sixgun. Nor was he particularly quick witted; he owed his post of marshal to his great strength and fistic ability rather than to quick wits. Right now he was well out of his depth.

"I've seen Tommy face down men who would eat Thompson. Why's he acting like that for?"

"Because of the gun. I remember Terry Ortega telling me about that gun. Tommy was just another cowhand until he bought it. Then he started to show how good he was with it. That was why you took him on as deputy, wasn't it?" Doc asked.

"Sure, I ain't any hand with a gun and Maisie wants me to quit being marshal and take over the cooking full time down at our place. So I picked me a man with a fast gun and with sense enough to know when to use it. I never saw Tommy act scared like this before."

"Confidence does strange things to a man, Biscuits," Doc said and he went to the window to look out, then returned and went on. "Tommy thought that it was owning Longley's gun that gave him confidence and made him good. Now he hasn't got Longley's gun he's scared."

"But that gun never belonged to Bad Bill," Waco objected.

"That doesn't matter, boy. I knew a dude one time. The boys told him a hoss was gentle. That dude walked up to the hoss, slapped it when it shied and got afork it. Rode it too. That hoss was a killer. The dude found out and when he went to try to ride it the next time he was scared. The hoss near to killed him."

"What're you getting at, Doc?" Biscuits inquired.

"Tommy's the same way. He thinks the gun made him what he is. Without it he's scared."

"Then I'll deputise some men and we'll run Thompson out of town as soon as he gets here."

"That won't do, Biscuits," Waco put in. He was looking down at the desk top. "This is Tommy's fight and as long as Thompson stacked against him alone, the town can't cut in. If you do deputise men, Tommy will be done as a lawman."

"What can we do?" Biscuits growled. "I ain't going to see Tommy killed."

"Leave it to me," Waco answered. "I know something that might work."

The other two knew Waco by now, knew him too well to ask any questions of him. Doc and Waco returned to their room at the hotel and the young Texan was silent, not saying anything until they were sitting on their beds. He looked up, "Sorry about this, Doc," he said, and walked out of the room.

The time was ten minutes to twelve and Biscuits stood by Doc Leroy outside the jail. Waco came towards them, a paper-wrapped object in his hand. He did not do more than greet them, then went inside, shutting the door behind him.

Tommy Melveny sat at the desk, his gunbelt with the empty holster laying before him. He was cleaning a shotgun and looked up at Waco.

"I know," he said. "I haven't got a chance."

"Not with a shotgun, against a man who can handle a Colt anything like well."

"It's my only chance."

"Wouldn't say that." Waco opened the paper wrappings and took out a white-handled Colt Civilian Peacemaker and holster. "You allow you was good with one of Bill Longley's guns, how do you reckon you'd be with one of Dusty Fog's?"

"Dusty Fog's gun?" There was reverence, almost, in Tommy's voice as he reached out and took the gun, looking down at its smooth blued, four and three-quarter inch barrel, the chamber, the hammer and the smooth, handfitting curve of the butt. "This is one of Dusty Fog's guns?"

"One of the brace he used at Tombstone," Waco replied.

Tommy hefted the gun, testing the feel in his hand; the look of worry was gone now. He knew that though Longley was fast, Dusty Fog was faster. He also knew that Waco was a very good friend of the Rio Hondo gun wizard, Dusty Fog. Getting to his feet he took up the gunbelt and removed the long holster, for it would not do for the shorter Civilian model gun. He slipped the new holster in place and dropped the gun into it, then strapped on his belt. He was trying the pigging thongs when he heard hoofbeats in the street outside.

"Tommy, Tommy Melveny, come on out here!" a voice yelled.

Tommy drew the gun, checked it was fully loaded and then holstered it and with his shoulders braced back stepped out on to the sidewalk. Waco came out after him, moving to one side.

Across the street Check Thompson looked at Tommy, then at the two Rangers and lastly at Biscuits, a ten gauge shotgun looking like a twig in his huge hand.

"Lot of backing you got there, Tommy boy," he said mockingly.

"You're not alone yourself," Tommy answered, glancing at the three men who formed a half-circle behind the gunman.

"The boys are only here to see the fun," Thompson replied. "They heard you'd got your gun bust and came along to see if it was right."

"It's right," Tommy's voice was as of old, not the worried, scared note of the night before. "Were they the three who attacked me?"

"Sure."

"Then I'm taking them in for assault."

Thompson felt uneasy; he knew how Tommy Melveny felt about that gun and was sure that without it the deputy would be afraid to come out and face him. Then he saw the gun in the holster.

"See you got a new gun, Tommy. Reckon it's as good as Longley's?"

"Better," Tommy answered, "it belonged to Dusty Fog."

Thompson's face was blank for a moment. He too knew the name and reputation of Dusty Fog. He also knew Waco was a friend of Dusty Fog, more than a friend, Waco had been like Dusty's younger brother.

Licking his lips, Check Thompson forced himself to make a decision. His hand dropped as he hissed, "You're a liar."

Tommy's hand went down in a fast move, closing on the grip of the gun and bringing it out in a flickering blur of movement. The gun jerked back in his palm as he brought it into line and, through the swirling smoke, saw Thompson rocking over backwards, gun half out of his holster.

The three men who'd come to town with Thompson looked down at the body, then up at Waco who was starting forward. They made a concerted rush for their horses, tearing the reins free and going into the saddles faster than a Comanche taking out after a white-eye scalp. Before Waco was off the sidewalk all three were tearing out of town at a full gallop.

People crowded out from where they'd been standing watching. Tommy Melveny shoved the gun back into leather and turned to Waco.

"I'd like to buy the gun."

"Why, there's plenty more like it at Neil's Hardware store."

"Not like this one it's—"

"A new gun. I bought it for Doc's birthday and it's never been fired before."

Tommy lifted the gun from leather and looked down at it again. Now he could see that this was no well-used firearm; it was new, brand new.

"But you said it belonged to Dusty Fog," he finally got out.

"Sure and you believed it. The same as you believed the other belonged to Bad Bill Longley. Tell you something, ole Bad Bill never owned a Peacemaker in his life. He used the 1860 Army gun. That one you owned couldn't have been his."

"Why didn't you tell me sooner?"

"You wouldn't have believed me. That was why I brought the gun just before you needed it. I didn't want you examining it too closely. Now do you see there's nothing to that idea that the gun makes you fast."

Tommy squared back his shoulders. In that moment he changed from a boy to a man. He took the gun from his holster, handing it back to Waco then laughing, he started to walk away.

"Where're you going boy?" Biscuits asked.

Looking back over his shoulder, Tommy grinned broadly. "To buy me a gun."